PRAISE FOR
RON FAUST

"Faust's prose is as smooth and bright as a sunlit mirror."
—*Publishers Weekly*

"Hemingway is alive and well and writing under the name Ron Faust."
—Ed Gorman, author of *Night Kills*

"Faust is one of our heavyweights . . . you can't read a book by Ron Faust without the phrase 'major motion picture' coming to mind."
—Dean Ing, *New York Times* bestselling author of *The Ransom of Black Stealth One*

"Faust writes of nature and men like Hemingway, with simplicity and absolute dominance of prose skills."
—Bill Granger, award-winning author of *Hemingway's Notebook*

"He looms head and shoulders above them all—truly the master storyteller of our time. Faust will inevitably be compared to Hemingway."
—Robert Bloch, author of *Psycho*

NOWHERE TO RUN

RON FAUST

TURNER

Turner Publishing Company
200 4th Avenue North • Suite 950 • Nashville, Tennessee 37219
445 Park Avenue • 9th Floor • New York, New York 10022

www.turnerpublishing.com

NOWHERE TO RUN

Cover design: Glen M. Edelstein
Book design: Glen M. Edelstein

Library of Congress Cataloging-in-Publication Data

Faust, Ron.
  Nowhere to run / Ron Faust.
     pages ; cm.
  ISBN 978-1-62045-434-3
  I. Title.
  PS3556.A98N69 2013
  813'.54--dc23

                              2013005051

Printed in the United States of America
13 14 15 16 17 18 19 0 9 8 7 6 5 4 3 2 1

NOWHERE TO RUN

ONE

"*Mariposa. Quiero ver tu cara.*"

She did not understand.

A hot sea wind had been blowing for three days and now it blew dust and bits of paper along the street and ballooned the skirt of the girl's djellaba. She smoothed the skirt with her palms and looked up at him. She was slender, and perhaps pretty; he could not tell for sure because of the veil, although he knew that her eyes were large and blue and had a slight oval slant. Her eyes seemed illuminated from within. They were bright and metallic with craziness.

"*Mariposa, venga aqui.*"

David was sitting cross-legged on the small second-floor balcony. The street below was a narrow, sloping canyon; gray paving stones, sun-bleached pastel-colored buildings without lanes or alleys between, a pale strip of sky overhead. He looked down at her through the twisted wrought-iron bars of the railing.

"Take off your veil," he said.

She seemed startled by the simple command. She looked up at him and there was something like fear in her crazy eyes. She stiffened and her eyes changed: surprise, fear, appeal—he saw, or believed he saw, all of them in her eyes.

The wind gusted again, carrying the fishy sea odors of plankton and mangrove swamp and sun-rotted kelp. The girl's skirt ballooned again, filled like a parachute. She spilled the air from it by rubbing her palms down the front of her thighs.

"Why are you wearing that costume?" David asked.

The effects of his fever swelled and diminished like the wind. For brief periods he felt completely normal, but then he was carried away. All temporal and spatial perceptions were distorted. Time ceased being linear and became a kind of mosaic in which certain areas remained blank and others were filled with color and action.

"What is your name?" he asked her.

"Strawberry Lassitude," she said. Her voice was a thin, passive, flute note.

David decided to go down into the street. He got up, went into his room, but then a surge of fever lifted him onto a vertiginous crest, held him there for a moment and then rolled him down into the trough.

He sat on the floor and looked around. He had the feeling that two years were missing from his life. The room, his quarters for most of that time, was now strange to him. There was no real furniture; a seven-foot cardboard wardrobe, straw mats on the tile floor, a couple of boat cushions, a blanket, a charcoal brazier, a tea kettle and skillet, earthenware pots, a ten-gallon jug of *agua pura*—he could not believe that this was his home.

He drank a glass of water and went to sleep in the heat and wind.

He dreamed of a diamond sun, many faceted and with a hard diamond light. Little flames, each no bigger than the flare of a match, erupted all over his body and as he walked he had to slap them out continually. He looked up at the sky and chanted *Rain, rain, rain!* and finally the diamond sun turned black and there was a bolt of luminous black lightning and the sky was ripped open. Rain obliquely streaked down and hissed on the hot stones. Steam began to rise, spiraling upward in twists that grew larger and larger until they were great black columns supporting the sky. They began spinning like tornado funnels. Sweat poured from his body. Each inhalation sucked hot mist into his lungs. The heat closed in, exerting a pressure as in deep water—he could not breathe. The rain turned into blood. And the steam was a blood-red color and moving more slowly through the air, billowing and mushrooming with a liquid viscosity.

When he awoke it was night and the girl was gone.

He went up on the roof and looked down over the village to the sea. At night the lights of town and of boats at anchor seemed to be merely reflections of the stars. He felt immersed in a light-flecked, galactic calm. The village (it was called El Jardin de los Reyes—Garden of the Kings) was a confused, angular design of moonlight and shadow which cascaded down the steep hills toward the sea. The sea itself was indigo except for a finely etched crescent of moonlight on top of each wave. It all looked like a very good, meticulously shaded aquatint.

David annihilated himself in the night for an hour and then returned to his room.

Early the next morning he was walking down the steep path to the sea when he saw the girl. She was standing on a ferny plateau above the beach, playing a harmonica. Her djellaba rippled in the wind. He came down the trail's last switchback and paused.

"Hello."

She lowered the harmonica, tugged at her veil. "Good morning."

He hesitated. "Listen, do you need anything? Food, a place to stay, a little money?"

"No."

"Where are your friends?"

"They went to Guatemala. The police told us to leave."

"Why didn't you go with your friends?"

"The wind told me to stay."

"What?"

"The sun told me that I was not ready."

"Yeah," David said.

"What is your sign?"

"Pardon?"

"Your sign, your sign," she said impatiently.

"Oh. Pisces."

She nodded slowly. "I knew it, yes."

"What is your name?"

"Strawberry Lassitude."

"No, I mean your real name."

"That is my real name. It came to me in the night."

"Oh, Christ," he said. Her honeyed voice and her crazy eyes and the wary, coiled-spring intensity of her posture tired him. These flute-voiced fey mystics actually admired their madness, sought it, smugly practiced it, and so of course spiraled deeper and deeper into it.

He started down the path, then stopped and turned. "Listen, you should wear shoes."

"Why?"

"There is a lot of hookworm around here."

"What is that?"

"A type of worm. They're in the feces of infected animals and humans. They enter your body through your feet, breed, circulate through the bloodstream. They hook onto the walls of your arteries—that's why they're called hookworm."

"Were they made by God?"

"What?"

"Hookworms were made by God too, weren't they?"

"I suppose. I suppose," David said, and he walked on down the path.

That night the girl appeared in the doorway of his room. She was carrying a paper bag of brown rice and asked him to boil some of it for her. She talked rapidly, almost constantly, but did not make much sense. David cooked the rice over the charcoal brazier along with a fish he had speared that afternoon. She shared her rice with him but refused to eat any of the fish, nor would she accept beer or coffee. He did not have any tea. She ate without removing her veil, delicately lifting the lower edge with her right hand while using the fork with her left. He saw that her teeth were good, her lips red and heavy.

"In a previous life I was the favorite wife in the harem of a great sheik," she said.

"Yeah?"

There was long hair on her calves, and she did not smell clean—sweat mingled with patchouli oil.

She asked if she could rest for a while. Of course, David said. She stretched out on a straw mat. She wanted to know if David wanted to stretch out beside her and rest too. No. She talked drowsily for a time and then she slept.

David went up onto the roof for half an hour, and when he returned, the girl was still sleeping. He quietly leaned over and lifted the veil. He half expected to see some scar or deformity, but her face was ordinary, almost pretty. There was only a small plum-colored birthmark on her left cheek; it was roughly heart shaped and no bigger than a dime.

The girl suddenly opened her eyes and screamed. She screamed three times, short, shrill bursts, and then she began weeping. She covered the birthmark with her palm and cried and sobbed with an anguish that confused him. He had never seen anyone suffer this way. Her misery, and the noises expressing it, were so intolerable to David that she hardly seemed human anymore and he thought of killing her as one might kill a dog that had been hit by a car.

She could not be consoled. She wept for a long time and then, exhausted and pale, graceless, she got her bag of rice and went out the door and down the stairway.

David walked out onto the balcony. The girl stood below, clutching her paper bag, sobbing harshly, looking up and down the street, and then she started off into the shadows.

"Sorry," he called. "Really. Strawberry?"

TWO

A small gray lizard was spread-eagled against the east wall of his room. David thought that there was something sacrificial in the lizard's cruciform pose, its immobility. It had tiny webbed hands, warty skin, and eyes mounted in blunt cones with each working independent of the other. Gyroscopic eyes. An iridescent fly went too close and the lizard's tongue unrolled like a paper snake—a miss.

David heard footsteps on the stairs, silence as his visitor paused on the landing, and then there was a slow, heavy rapping on the door. The lizard scurried down the hall and vanished into a hole between two tiles.

A heavy-fisted pounding that threatened to splinter the door panel. *"Policia!"*

David got up, crossed the room and opened the door.

"Vigil," the man said, emphasizing the throaty, aspirant *g* so that his name did not sound like the usual *vee-heel*, but closer to *vee-keel*. He showed David an ornate gold shield that contained an eagle with a snake in its beak—an Aztec, and now national symbol. The shield identified him as a captain in the Mexican Federal Police. He was tall, about David's height of six feet, and thin, with a narrow, pock-scarred face and kinky brownish hair and protuberant green eyes. He waited, staring at David.

"I'm sorry. Come in, Captain."

The policeman walked slowly to the center of the room and turned in a three-hundred-and-sixty degree circle, looking at everything. "Very . . . bohemian," he said with evident distaste.

"I have coffee," David said. "Or, if you'd prefer a drink . . . "

"I smell patchouli oil," Vigil said, staring at David with an expression somewhere between irony and contempt. "Do you anoint yourself with that foul-smelling grease?"

"I had a guest last night. She uses it."

"I thought perhaps you used it as an aftershave. Or for insect repellent. No doubt you're troubled by vermin here."

David started to say that he was troubled by vermin at this very moment, but he bit off the words; he wouldn't get away with it, not with this cop. The federal police had as much power as they elected to exercise.

David walked past him and opened the wood-louvered doors which led out onto the balcony; sunlight burst in, flooded across the floor, and splashed halfway up the back wall. The captain stood chest-deep in light.

"I usually keep the place closed up at this time of day," David said. "The heat, and the exhaust smells."

"Yes, yes," Vigil said impatiently, and then he waded through the light to a wooden crate in the corner (David used it for a table) and picked up the small obsidian knife. He tested it with his thumb.

"I wonder how many human chests this dull knife hacked open," he said.

"None. It's a fake. I made it myself. I had hoped to sell it to a tourist."

"Yes? It looks authentic. Did you know that it has been estimated that when the Aztecs dedicated their temple of war, the priest sacrificed twenty thousand human beings?"

"I didn't know that."

"Twenty thousand hearts cut out, from dawn to dusk in a single day. Incredible. With knives such as these. How could it be?" And then with irony: "I am not questioning the slaughter in a moral way, you understand, but"—he held up the knife—"but only the technological aspects."

"Sort of Third World pluck, isn't it?" David said.

"The Aztecs were cruel, but they were great too. Very great."

"They made the sun rise on time," David said.

Vigil stared contemptuously at David for a time and then he suddenly grinned. "That's very funny," he said without mirth. "You are a funny man." His teeth were long and crooked and spiky. He had a ferocious wolf-grin. His green eyes bulged. For a few seconds he appeared more animal than human, and then his artificial smile vanished and he was just an ordinary man in an ordinary blue suit. A great party trick, David thought. He didn't know if this man was a dangerous lunatic or a harmless clown.

"I myself am part Aztec, a small part," Vigil said quietly. "A few of my distant relatives still speak Nahuatl. I don't know that tongue, I'm afraid. I speak only Spanish and English—the English poorly."

"No, you speak English quite well."

"Thank you. Well, I studied English in school here. And I later attended the Police Science course at Northwestern University, and after that went to the FBI Academy." He paused and then there was another change of mood, and with mockery he said, "I was a legal resident of the United States during that period."

David waited.

"Let me see your tourist card."

"I don't have one."

"Then show me your resident papers."

David shook his head.

Vigil tried to appear shocked. "You are an illegal alien?"

"You know I am."

"Yes, I know you are."

David relaxed; it was out now, the cop was here to shake him down for a little money. Maybe he was late with his car payment or his wife wanted a new pair of shoes.

"I'm poor at the moment, Captain, but if you'll give me a few days I'm sure I can—"

"Shut up." Vigil flicked his fingers, dismissing the offer of a bribe as if brushing lint off his jacket.

"Do you know this strange child, this Raspberry Lassitude?"

"Strawberry."

"What?"

"Strawberry. She calls herself Strawberry Lassitude, not Raspberry."

Vigil's mouth twitched in sour amusement. "I see. I had the wrong berry. Well, do you know her?"

"Yes."

"How well?"

"Not well."

"Well enough to know her true name?"

"No."

"You know her only as Strawberry Lassitude?"

"That's right."

"Tell me, do you call her Strawberry? Or Miss Lassitude? Never mind. Do you know her this well?" Vigil closed his right hand into a fist and pumped it up and down several times.

"No."

"She was alone with you in this room last night, wasn't she?"

"That doesn't mean . . . Look, she ate here at about nine o'clock. She left before ten."

"Ten o'clock. Are you certain?"

"Absolutely. You can ask the people who live on the street. She made a disturbance and someone probably noticed. They could tell you that she left here alone."

"And you didn't *poder*—not even a little?"

"No."

And now again, without transition, Vigil abruptly changed the subject and mood. "How can you live like this?" he asked furiously.

David confused and wary, involuntarily took a step backward. "Like what?"

Vigil threw out a hand, sliced the air. "Like this," he said angrily, bitterly.

David looked around his room. "It's clean."

"Clean!"

"I live no worse than most of the people in this area."

"No, you live better than most of them."

"Well then, what—"

"Shut up." Vigil paced back and forth across the room several times and then, incredibly, he smiled faintly and said, "What do you have to drink?"

"Coffee."

"No, to *drink*."

"Rum."

"Fine, let us have a rum then."

"Coke?" David asked. "Lime juice and sugar?"

"Just rum if it has quality."

David poured two ounces of rum into a glass and handed it to the policeman.

"Aren't you going to drink with me?"

"Yes." He splashed rum into another glass.

"No, what I meant—you live this way when you do not have to, while the others, our poor, the poor everywhere, have no choice."

"I have no choice at the moment."

"This nostalgia of mud that you Americans have— you so love to play the game of poverty. You romanticize ignorance and deprivation."

"You aren't talking about me," David said.

"This poor child, Strawberry Lassitude. Her friends. The others we see. Playing games, pretending, idealizing the crude and backward. But you always have the machines behind you. The machines are there waiting when you sicken of the nineteenth century. There they stand, oiled and gleaming, waiting, for when your agrarian fantasy and primitive tribal fantasy and noble craftsman fantasy have failed."

"Really, Captain, you aren't talking about me."

Vigil nodded slowly. "I sometimes embarrass myself with my passion and eloquence. That kind of thing sounds perfectly natural in Spanish, but in English . . . "

David smiled. "It sounded glorious in English."

"Your sick, pathetic Strawberry Lassitude is dead. A fisherman found her body this morning on the rocks at the base of the cliffs."

"Suicide?"

"Certainly, if we can accept the hypothesis that she strangled herself an hour or so before hurling her body off the cliff."

"Murdered."

"You're very quick. We don't have a pathologist here, but Dr. Pacheco performed the autopsy. You know Dr. Pacheco?"

"Yes."

"What did she eat for dinner?"

"Just rice."

"And what time did she eat?"

"About nine."

"And she left here at ten o'clock?"

"Around ten, yes. I'm sure that if you ask my landlady, my neighbors, they will confirm it."

"Because she created a disturbance."

"Yes."

"Why?"

"I don't—she was very emotional, unbalanced."

"Surely there must have been some provocation."

"I lifted her veil. She had a birthmark on her cheek—I don't know. Look, I didn't hurt her."

"Did she resist when you lifted her veil?"

"She was asleep."

Vigil flashed his avid, wolfish grin.

"I know it sounds odd."

"She slept here."

"For maybe twenty minutes."

"How often did she come here for a nap?"

"She was never in this room before last night. I hardly knew her. I cooked her rice for her, she ate it, she slept for a while and then awakened when I lifted her veil. And she went a little crazy."

"Where are her friends?"

"She told me that the police had ordered them to leave town."

"I know that, I am the police. Where did they go?"

"To Guatemala, she said."

"She should have gone with them."

"Yes."

"Why didn't she?"

"I don't know."

"Well, the Guatemala authorities will find her friends and perhaps learn this Strawberry's real name, and her city. And no doubt we can locate her parents and inform them that their daughter was a victim of crime, which they might very well have anticipated. And, I suppose, they will decline to come here and claim the body, or even pay the funeral expenses. Or else they'll come here and weep like saints."

Vigil sipped his rum and stared calmly, levelly at David. "Well, she's dead. Murdered. What do you think of it?"

"It's terrible."

"No, I mean what do you really think?"

"I'm thinking that if you aren't a good, straight cop I might be in serious trouble."

Vigil smiled faintly. "And what do you feel?"

"Fear."

"For yourself?"

"Yes."

"And for the girl?"

"Pity."

"What did you feel for her when she was alive?"

"The same, I suppose—pity."

Vigil nodded. "Perhaps."

"What about you?" David asked. "What do you feel?"

Vigil stared intently into David's eyes for a time and then he walked a few feet away and turned. "Mexico is a violent country, like the United States. We talked about the Aztecs. You know about the Conquest, our Revolutions. Murder is frequent, crimes of passion. But, do you know, we rarely encounter the dark, perverted sex crimes and mutilations that you'll find in the Anglo-Saxon societies. Do you understand what I'm saying?"

"Yes. You believe that an American killed the girl."

"Exactly."

"I'm not a policeman . . . "

"I know that."

"But if I were, I wouldn't automatically exclude ninety-five percent of the local population."

"You would be a mediocre policeman then, because one must automatically exclude ninety-five percent of the population before beginning one's inquiries. I arbitrarily exclude all women from this investigation. I exclude all children below the age of—say fourteen. I exclude all the arthritic, passionless old men. I exclude all those whom I know, or feel, to be incapable of such an act. I exclude all those citizens who have no history of crime, especially crimes of violence. I exclude those who are so seriously handicapped as to be virtually immobile. I exclude overt homosexuals—they generally kill men or boys, not females. I exclude, I exclude, I exclude. I must reduce the field to the probables."

"Maybe the killer was a transient."

"Possible. But for now I exclude all transients."

"All right, but to say that the killer is an American is ridiculous. You might be wrong."

"Of course."

"You might be way off the track."

Vigil nodded. "Yes, yes," he said impatiently, "but is there any reason why I should now be questioning the old lady who sells ices on the corner or the mayor rather than you, David Rhodes?"

"I guess not."

"If you did it, and confess to me now, I can promise you that you will be out of prison in five years."

"I didn't do it."

"There is considerable pressure on me. I can't take very long with this. We can bargain."

David shook his head.

"Mexico City wants this cleared up quickly. You people! Your country is at least as violent as mine. But if one American is killed in Mexico, one million American tourists stay home with their money."

"It would be good for the tourism if an American were arrested for the murder of another American, wouldn't it?"

"It would be perfect," he said with his fierce, canine grin.

"One million tourists."

"Many millions of dollars."

"Vigil—Captain—I didn't do it."

Vigil lifted his glass and drained the rum. He stared at David. Stared, and then suddenly in another queer paroxysm of rage, he hurled his glass against the wall;

it exploded with a dull popping noise, and splinters of glass sprayed out into the sunlight, flashing, and then rattling dryly on the tiles. His eyes bulged, his face was swollen and dark with blood.

And then in a hushed tone, a near whisper, he said, "If it was you, tell me now. If it was you and you wait . . . Christ help you, man."

These sudden changes of mood, switches of persona, confused David. It seemed that Vigil was two men, a compact Mutt and Jeff team, the nice cop and the mean cop in one. And David, knowing better, found himself liking and trusting the gentle Vigil while despising the other. It seemed to him that his own personality was splitting down the center in order to accommodate the two Vigils; he responded with sympathy, or a nearly equal hatred.

"We can deal," the gentle Captain Vigil said. "Or I can get you and break you on my own," the cruel Vigil said.

After he had gone, David stood quietly in the center of the room, sipping his rum, thinking, and then he turned and threw his glass against the wall. Another dull explosion, a shower of glass splinters. It made him feel slightly better to ape Vigil's act. It was, for an instant, like sharing his power.

THREE

Brown pelicans folded their wings and made clumsy crosswind landings in the troughs between waves. The tops of the coconut palms were greenly incandescent in the sunlight but it was cool and dim in the shade below. Here, there was a soothing opacity, a rippling underwater sheen, while beyond the grove of trees the morning sun glazed the air and slowly devoured the shadows it had created.

David was sitting beneath a tree, trying to make a sand sculpture of a stray dog. The dog was sleeping nearby in a splash of sun-marbled shade. Its ears and tail twitched at flies. The dog was part dachshund and part something quite different and David didn't know if the trouble with his sculpture was due to his inexpert hand or the dog's ancestry—the proportions were all wrong.

He heard Dr. Pacheco before he saw him: there was a shout, half lost in the sounds of wind and surf, "Dah-veed, Dah-veed, it's me, your resurrector!"

Pacheco was sixty feet away, grinning, walking bow-legged along where the surf washed the sand with an iridescent froth. He wore a straw hat, khaki shorts, and an orange life preserver. The woman called Esther walked a dozen paces behind.

Pacheco yelled again, and the dog jerked awake, looked toward him for a moment, and then fell back with a snuffling groan.

David watched them approach. Pacheco was very short and thin, about five feet three inches tall and weighing no more than a hundred and twenty pounds. His head was large in relation to his body and made him look dwarfish. His jaw was underslung and when he smiled you could see that his lower incisors projected beyond the uppers; it was a barracuda smile. Now, breathing deeply, he stopped a few feet away and looked down at David.

"We should embrace," he said. "If you weren't from such a cold, barbaric people we would embrace."

"How are you, Paco?"

"That isn't the question. The question is how are you?"

"I'm all right."

Pacheco leaned over to look at the sand sculpture. He looked at the sculpture and then at the dog. "Not too bad," he said. "But a little stiff. It looks like a dead dog and not a sleeping one. You agree that there is a difference?"

"Some."

"Some indeed."

The woman arrived. She nodded at David, exhaled a long hissing sigh and set down a carton of beer.

"Hello, Esther," David said.

"Hi, sweets. How are you?"

"Open a beer for our friend David," Pacheco said. "And one for me and one for you." He sat cross-legged on the sand. "So. So, David, the police—indifferent as usual to the public welfare—have left you free to prowl."

"So far."

"You, David, are the deceptively soft-spoken maniacal killer in our midst, and only I, the compassionate and awesomely intelligent Dr. Pacheco, suspect that a hormonal deficiency has turned your heart to stone and your brain to murder."

"There he goes," Esther said, passing out the cold cans of Tecate beer.

"No woman is safe until the evil monster is subdued and psychoanalyzed."

"Leave him alone," the woman said.

"What do you mean 'leave him alone'?" Pacheco replied. "I am his physician and confessor and resurrector."

"Just hush now, Francisco."

"He's a psychopath, a slayer of rice-eating hippie girls."

"Oh, God," she said. "One of these days someone is going to break your ugly jaw, Francisco."

"Certainly. But not David. Even Americans don't break the jaw of their resurrector."

Pacheco lay flat on the sand, hands linked behind his head, blinking up at the writhing palm fronds. "My boat is back in the water. Do you want to go sailing tomorrow?"

"What time?"

"In the morning."

"I have to give a tennis lesson to Harry Rudd tomorrow morning."

"The day after, then."

"I'll think about it."

"Are you able to make decisions?"

"I'm about to make one particular decision, Paco."

Pacheco laughed. "That sounded like a threat. Do you know what I think? I think that you are afraid to go sailing with me because of what happened that day when I had to resurrect you."

"Jesus!" Esther said. "Just what is all this resurrection stuff?"

"You don't know? I never told you?"

"You never tell me anything except 'do this' and 'do that.'"

"It was wonderful. We were sailing about six months ago and David drowned. First you must understand that I run a sloppy ship, ropes, junk everywhere. We were flying the spinnaker and David was returning to the cockpit when he tripped over the end of the jib sheet. Regard the jib sheet as a rope, Esther. Now, it isn't extraordinary to trip over a rope. It isn't extraordinary to fall overboard. But it is nearly miraculous to trip over a rope and fall overboard with the loose end of the rope fiendishly wrapped around your ankle. That implies a nonhuman intelligence at work; the rope thinking like a python; or perhaps one of those sinister intercessions of God."

"Well, he didn't drown, Francisco. He's sitting here right now."

Pacheco was silent for a time, hating her, and then he sat up and took another can of beer. "Talk about nonhuman nonintelligence."

"Well, what happened?"

"I was dragged through the water backwards and almost upside down," David said. "I passed out after a minute or so. I was unconscious by the time Paco got the boat stopped and me aboard."

"Drowned?"

David smiled. "Damned close to it."

"Dead," Pacheco said.

"Medically dead?"

"What other kind of dead do you know about, Esther? Tell me and I'll write a paper for Lancet."

"Paco tells me that I wasn't breathing, and he couldn't detect a heartbeat."

"My God! What did you do, Francisco?"

"I thumped him on the sternum half a dozen times and then performed mouth-to-mouth resurrection. It was awful. I detected unknown homosexual tendencies in myself."

"But that's resuscitation, not resurrection," Esther said.

"Esther, you ignorant sow of Ohio, I know what I am saying. I speak this barbaric tongue better than you do."

"Abuse, that's all you know how to talk."

"Paco the resurrector. I am something, am I not, my friend?"

"You are something, all right," David said.

"You haven't thanked me yet this week."

"I'm tired of thanking you. Send me a bill."

"You don't have any money. You are my one and only charity case. Anyway, what is the going fee for resurrection?"

"Francisco is the most selfish man I've ever met," Esther said.

"Shut up, you doleful, wearisome bitch. The world requires cheapskates and fascists."

"Are you a fascist, Paco?" David asked.

"Sometimes, when I meet people who hate fascism."

"What are you, then?"

"Politically, I am an anarchist."

"And?"

"Morally, I am an anarchist. Aren't I, Esther?"

"Intellectually?" David asked.

"Intellectually, I am an anarchist. Scientifically, I am an anarchist."

"What else?"

"What else? Well, aesthetically I am an anarchist too. I like your sand sculpture and your nonexistent verse—silence is the poetry of today. Physically, I am an anarchist, as you can see."

He laughed. "I guess I am an anarchist in all ways. I didn't know that when embarking on this voyage of self-discovery. How strange. I feel strangely whole, strangely integrated now. I think I shall be a happy—even giddy—man from this moment on."

"What a goof," Esther said.

"And what are you, David?"

"I don't know."

"You are a romantic."

"No. Not any more."

"Yes, you are. I say you are a romantic."

David shook his head.

"How do you see yourself? That is, when you get an image of yourself, what are you doing?"

He shrugged.

"Killing helpless females, perhaps? That isn't exactly romantic in the modern pop-song sense, but there is a—"

"Francisco!" Esther cried. "Will you stop this vicious nonsense!"

"I am his resurrector."

Esther stood up and brushed the sand off of the back of her shorts.

"Sit down," David said. "I can handle Paco."

"You only think you can," Pacheco said.

"He's such a dirty, mean little bastard!" she said furiously. "You don't know what he's like sometimes, when we're alone."

"Esther," Pacheco said. "You only think you have the right sentiments. You learned sentiments the same way you learned the multiplication tables. You are a dreary old sow, Esther, and I am tired of you."

She turned sharply and walked away. She went through the deep sand and when she was almost to the water she stumbled and nearly fell. She recovered, straightened, and resumed walking parallel to the sea, but she was limping slightly now.

"Ruined her exit," Pacheco said.

"She was right. You are a mean bastard."

"Of course I am."

"Esther is nice."

"She is a rich, dull-witted Ohio widow. You think she's nice because she likes you."

David opened a can of beer, took a drink. "Paco, loan me three hundred dollars, will you?"

"The only way I can maintain our precarious friendship is by pretending that I didn't hear that."

"I think I'd better get out of this town."

"Going home?"

"No, I can't."

"That's right, you've been indicted in the States. They'll put you in jail. And if you stay here you might go to jail too." He lowered his voice again. "Today police announced that the baby-faced killer was faced with a dilemma . . . "

"I don't have a baby face," David said.

"The fiendish killer denied having a baby face."

"Paco, you don't really believe that I hurt that girl."

"She was more than hurt, she was murdered."

"You know that I didn't do it."

"I know nothing of the sort. I don't *think* you killed her, but that's something else, isn't it?"

"Vigil believes I did it."

"I know."

"That Vigil is a strange man."

"A very tough cop."

"At times he seems to be a shy, gentle man, and then he suddenly flies off into a terrific rage."

Pacheco grinned.

"He threw a glass against my wall. Is he acting when he does things like that?"

"I've often wondered."

"I told him that the girl left my room at about ten o'clock. It's true. If he checks, asks around . . . "

Pacheco finished his beer, threw the can aside.

"What did you find out in the autopsy?"

"I'm not a pathologist."

"Still . . . "

"She died several hours after eating the rice—say midnight or one o'clock. She was strangled and then some time later thrown off the cliff. She had been dead for an hour or two when she hit the rocks."

"So the one who killed her later took her body down to the cliffs and threw it over."

"Perhaps."

"What else, Paco?"

"She'd had sexual intercourse that night. There was sperm. Did you screw her, David?"

"No."

"Well, if you did we'll find out."

"How?"

"I've put some sperm on a slide. Have you ever seen human sperm through a microscope? They look like tadpoles. With a strong enough scope you can make out their features. If they all look like you, David . . . ”

"Very funny."

"There is one beer left. Do you want it?"

"Yes, thanks."

"I was just being courteous. It's mine and you were supposed to refuse."

"Listen, Paco, really—will you loan me three hundred dollars?"

"No. I resurrect you, that ought to be enough. No. Three hundred dollars is a couple ounces of decent caviar. Three hundred dollars is a new mainsail. Three hundred dollars is a dissolute weekend in Mexico City. Buzz off, sonny, I thought we were friends."

"Okay, Paco."

"Here, I'll take your pulse. Free."

"Never mind."

"Stick out your tongue."

"Ah."

"Healthy tongue."

"Paco, don't tell anyone around here that I'm a fugitive."

"I won't, unless you have the bad taste to ask me for a loan again."

"There are moralists in the American community."

"There are moralists everywhere, patriots and moralists. We must remember to behave hypocritically."

David stood up.

"Where are you going?"

"To town."

"Why don't you come swimming with me first?"

"No."

"I was going to try it without my life jacket but not if I have to go out there alone. I doubt if I could resurrect myself. Sailing the day after tomorrow?"

"I'll let you know."

David was thirty yards away when Pacheco called, "If you see Esther, kill her for me."

FOUR

The next morning he gave a tennis lesson to Harry Rudd and afterward they lunched on the terrace. They each had two bottles of beer before lunch and then started drinking daiquiris. Beyond the low, stone, terrace wall, the green hills tumbled down to the sea. The day was hot and almost completely overcast; some boiling black clouds had swallowed the sun and they had watched a shadow sail over the sea and up the beach, up the hills and over the house. All the colors faded, the brilliant yellows and blues and greens and reds, and then everything had a faint brownish tint. There was a musty scent in the air.

Harry had gone into the house and now David watched as Ruben, the Rudds' gardener, pruned branches from a lime tree. He was a great gardener, Harry liked to say, because he could communicate with vegetables as an equal. Mrs. Rudd had fired Ruben half a dozen times and then hired him back; he won the annual spring garden show for her every year and so she endured his stupidity and lasciviousness.

31

"*Buenos días,* Ruben," David called.

"*Muy buenos días,*" Ruben said.

"Be nice to plants, Ruben, and plants will be nice to you," David said in English.

Ruben, not understanding, gave his slack-mouthed, goggle-eyed grin and pretended to amputate his genitals with the pruning shears.

David laughed and turned away. A few minutes later when Harry rejoined him, David said, "It looks like your man Ruben is going to trim that lime into matchsticks."

Harry looked down the terrace. "He knows what he's doing. Well, no, he doesn't know what he's doing I don't think, but it works."

"Has your wife fired him lately?"

"She's in the States, visiting the kids. She'll probably fire him when she gets back. She hates it when he explores his potential in public view."

David laughed.

"If he was an American, Ruben would pierce one ear and wear an earring, talk about pineal glands and karma and a hundred thousand punks would think he was a holy man. Ruben the savant. Political and cultural leaders would invite him to address their seminars. Fifteen-year-old girls would make pilgrimages of two thousand miles to worship at his verminous loins. But hell, the sappy bastard had the misfortune to be born Mexican and the other Mexicans think he's a repulsive idiot. Not even the goats will service him."

"A prophet is without honor . . . "

"That is the cruel truth."

"St. Ruben of the Vegetables. Have you seen him talk to the flowers, Harry?"

"You bet. He cups the flower to his lips and makes obscene phone calls. Nancy Cole filled his head with all that crap about sentient plants. Ruben sang to the bougainvillea and it died."

"You know, Harry, he might be dangerous."

"Dangerous? Ruben?"

"That small brain and that big itch."

"What are you thinking, kid? About that broad who was killed?"

"Yes."

"I don't know . . . "

"What is he, in his mid-thirties? A strong guy, with a powerful sex drive and no outlet."

"Oh, he has an outlet, all right."

"You know what I mean."

"Yeah, I know. Well, Christ, it's possible I guess."

"The cops think an American killed her."

Harry was silent for a time, then: "That figures. It's probably worth a few million American tourist dollars if an American is arrested."

"Captain Vigil thinks that I murdered her."

Rudd stared at him.

"She was at my place for a while on the night she was killed. She left around ten o'clock, and made a terrible fuss—crying, screaming."

"Jesus."

"Apparently she was killed a couple hours later. Vigil likes *me* for it."

"What was the crying and screaming about?"

David told him.

"This is depressing as hell. Well, Dave, I know you didn't do it, and anybody who tries to nail you for it is going to have to go through me."

"Thanks, Harry."

"The American community will be behind you."

"I hope you're right."

"Okay. Let's drop it for now. I'll see what I can do. Do you want another daiquiri?"

"Yes."

"Manuel!" Rudd shouted. *"Dos mas!* He's probably upstairs with the new maid. I suffer a daily crucifixion at the hands of my servants."

"You have my pity," David said.

"Well. How is my tennis game progressing?"

"Very slowly."

"Yeah? Who's fault is that, Mr. Instructor?"

"Yours. You constantly over-hit the ball, Harry. You just aren't a natural power player."

"The hell you say. I'm fifty-one years old and probably in the best physical condition of my life. I weigh two-oh-nine and I can bench press better than three hundred pounds. Look at this arm. And you tell me that I'm not a natural hitter."

"The Santistevan girl hasn't got the arm of a blacksmith but she can hit the ball harder than you."

"And why is that?"

"She has timing and a smooth, coordinated stroke. That's much more important than sheer strength."

"I want to ram the ball down their throats. I want to make tennis a blood sport."

"That's not your game."

"Am I ready to beat Charley Cole?"

"No."

"My form hasn't improved in three months. What am I paying you for?"

"Odd as it sounds, Harry, you're paying me to talk. You're paying to listen to me when I tell you something. Don't worry about form. Do it right, obey the sequence of action, and form will follow. Form, grace, even power—they come from doing a thing correctly."

"Great. And so where does that leave me?"

"If you want to hit the ball harder you can begin by swinging less hard."

"Davey, I like you, son, I really do. But sometimes you talk a lot of crap."

Manuel delivered two more daiquiris and took away the empty glasses.

"That Manuel kid makes a hell of a fine drink," Rudd said. "But I wish he wouldn't stalk silently around the place on the balls of his feet like a bullfighter."

The wind had risen. Palm fronds writhed and lashed like whips. Far below, the sea heaved furiously and spindrift, like white smoke, was torn from the tops of the waves.

"You talk a good game of tennis," Rudd said, "but I noticed that you ducked a match with Felix Mondragon when he was here last summer."

"I didn't duck a match, I was sick."

"Yeah, well a lot of people thought you were chicken."

"I can beat Mondragon."

"Don't kid yourself. He was on the Mexican Davis Cup team a couple of years ago."

"That should tell you about the level of competition down here. After Raul Ramirez there's just a bunch of guys like Mondragon."

"What are your credentials, pal?"

"I made the quarter finals in the National Junior tournament when I was sixteen. I was Conference singles champion my senior year in college. I played pro tennis for four years."

Rudd looked at him skeptically.

"It's true, Harry. A couple, three years ago I was ranked among the top one hundred and fifty tennis players in the world." David smiled. "One hundred and forty-seven to be precise."

"How come you never told me this before?"

"You never accused me of ducking Mondragon before."

"Pro, huh? Make any money?"

"Not much beyond expenses."

"One hundred and forty-seven isn't bad at all."

"I figured that I could probably make it into the top one hundred, maybe even the top fifty. If you get that high, and pick your tournaments, and find a good doubles partner, you can make a lot of money."

Harry smiled and slowly shook his head. "And you quit to write poetry."

"That's right." David had told people that he was a poet because that somehow seemed to explain his exile and poverty.

"Dumb. Well, kid, maybe you could have beaten Mondragon two years ago, but this is now."

"I can still beat him."

"Look, Dave, when we play a match you beat me 6-2, 6-3, sometimes even 6-4. I've never taken a set from you but I've won a lot of games. Now I know I'd never win a *game* from Felix."

"You'd never win a game from me if I played all out."

"You mean you've been loafing?"

"No, not loafing."

"What do you call it then?"

"Just making a game out of it, letting you play and work on your strokes. I just spin my serve in at about three-quarter speed; I rarely take the net; I don't hit any really hard ground strokes."

Harry Rudd drummed his fingers on the table. He looked at David out of the corner of his eye, looked away, glanced back. "Oh," he said, grinning. "Oh ho, listen, do you *honestly* believe that you can beat that *macho* hotdog Mondragon?"

David smiled. "He's pretty good."

"He was on the Mexican Davis Cup team."

"He's quick, very quick."

"A devious, left-handed dynamo," Rudd said.

"Not a great deal of power but he's always on the lines."

"A crisp slice backhand."

"He's temperamental, it might be easy to upset him, he might choke."

"He lives in Mexico City where it's cool. He's not used to this jungle humidity."

"A fine tennis player," David said. "I can beat him."

"David, son, this is no time for idle boasts."

"I-can-beat-him-Harold."

"For how much can you beat him?"

"All I've got, which isn't much."

"No one, I say no one, will believe that you can whip Felix Mondragon at tennis."

"I know."

"We can get odds. Two to one."

"Better than that."

"Times are bad," Harry Rudd said. "Inflation is ravaging the hemisphere. But I believe that I could scrape up five hundred dollars or so to place some sportsman-like wagers on such a match. Please, can you really beat the son of a bitch?"

"Yes."

"Who's talking, Dave or the daiquiris?"

"Dave Daiquiri, that's who."

"Three to one is fair, isn't it, Dave Daiquiri?"

"*Absolutamente.*"

"Four to one."

"*Por qué no?*"

"If you beat him I'll give you twenty percent of my winnings."

"*Mi patron,*" David crooned.

"If you lose I'll kick your ass all the way to Yucatán."

"*Qué lástima!*"

"You'll have to go into training, Dave Daiquiri."

"When is Mondragon coming here next?"

"Easter week, babe. Very soon."

"We'll hold secret workouts," David said.

"Secret workouts, oh boy! And you'll unveil your incredible serve?"

"Right. That's where I'll win, on my service game."

"Lay off the booze. Don't smoke. Remain chaste."

"You arrange the match, Harry. I'll appear reluctant and refuse to play him at first."

"Man, oh man, we'll sandbag this whole goddamned town. It's not just the money you understand, Dave Daiquiri—it's the joy of symbolically murdering your friends and relatives."

The rain started then, lightly at first, then slanting down hard, cold, and stinging. Pellets of rain drummed on the awning and swarmed over the swimming pool. Now a bolt of lightning bisected the sky and then those two halves were further divided by crooked prongs of light, and again, until the whole dark sky looked like a glowing spider web. A great, prolonged peal of thunder shook the hillside.

Running toward the house, David realized that he was more than a little drunk; and he was no longer certain that he could beat Felix Mondragon at tennis.

FIVE

It was late and David sat on the beach above the high-tide line. He smelled gasoline and turned: a crooked shadow was limping toward him.

"Chucho?" he said.

"*Qué tal,* Flaco?"

"Flaco yourself," David said.

Jesús Aguilar set down a large gasoline can and stretched his arms. "Oh, Christ, man, that there gas is so heavy. I carry it all the way from Llano Quemado."

"Where did you get it?"

"I stole it from a camper truck."

"Stupid."

"What stupid, man? I could have taken the whole truck." Chucho sat on the sand, remained motionless for a moment, then stretched out on his back.

"You're dumb," David said.

"Okay, okay. Shit."

"What have you been smoking, you dumb *pachuco?*"

"Hey, pachuco yourself, man. I got your *pachuco* stuff right here. *Mira.* Right here."

Chucho—the name was a diminutive to Jesús—was a thin, dark, fourteen year old with the whitest, most perfect teeth that David had ever seen. The boy seemed to regard his teeth as an indestructible all-purpose tool; he casually opened beer and cola bottles with them, cracked brazil nuts, splintered bones like a dog so that he could reach the marrow.

He had attended school for only a few years, could barely read and write, but he had a quick, predatory intelligence and a logic which transcended morality. When he stole money from the church poor-box he said, "Hey, man, I'm poor, ain't I? They never *give* me nothing." He was a one-boy socialist army, trying in his own way to equalize the wealth. Chucho was poor but David did not believe that he would always remain poor. The kid ignored all slogans and relied on observation. He was totally cynical, but even so he seemed to genuinely like people, even fools, especially fools it sometimes appeared. He was a cheerful cynic, unlike Dr. Pacheco who was a bitter cynic. David figured that the boy was cheerful because he'd never had the opportunity to be an idealist. Chucho accepted the world, the way things were, in the same uncritical way that a fish accepts water. It was his environment, that's all.

"How is your sex life, Flaco?"

"Looking down."

"Maria Cristina is home."

"She is?"

"Maybe the sex will improve. That Maria Cristina—hey, 'Mano, that is some beautiful lady."

"Let's get going," David said.

"Hey, Flaco, why'd you kill that poor little girl, huh? Didn't nobody ever say to you that you don't throw them away when you finish?"

"Where did you hear that I had anything to do with it?"

"It's all over this whole town."

"Jesus Christ!"

"I tell them Flaco didn't do it."

"Thanks a lot."

"Did you ever screw her, man?"

"Chucho . . . "

"I did. Three times. I saw her on the beach one time and we—"

"Shut up."

"Okay, okay, I didn't, but I almost did. We talked, you know, and later she lets me kiss her and play with her. But she says no when I try to put it in. And then she starts yelling, man. I got out of there fast."

"Is this true?"

"I swear."

"When was this?"

Chucho was quiet, then: "Two nights before you throw her down to the rocks. Hey, you didn't have to do that—they ain't dis-dispo-*como se dice?*"

"Disposable."

"Right."

"You'd better not tell anyone about that."

"I just did."

"Don't tell anyone else."

"I know, man, I'm smart. That Vigil would take me away and pull out all my teeth until I say I kill her."

"Look, you're always out on the streets. You say you see and hear everything. Maybe you can get an idea of who might have done it."

"I got ideas about that already. Pacheco kill her."

"Doctor Pacheco?"

"Sure, man, he's crazy. I see that girl come out of Pacheco's clinic late one night."

"He was probably treating her for something."

"At night, man? Ten, eleven at night he is treating her?"

"When was this?"

"I don't know. Maybe three, four days before you choke her."

David stood up. "Let's go, dummy."

"Listen, 'Mano, why don't we forget them lobsters this night?"

"I need the money."

"The hotels, they don't pay good."

"Good enough. I don't even have the money to buy an egg tomorrow morning."

"We could break into the Nicholson house, man. They gone to Guadalajara."

"No."

"I can open the door, 'Mano. I been practicing on all the locks on the street."

"The dogs would eat us alive."

"No, man, I been feeding them dogs. I throw meat over the fence and they smell me."

"What about the servants?"

"They be up the stairs, sleeping."

"Oh, for Christ's sake, Chucho."

"Well, you got to take chances, man."

David picked up his duffel bag. "Let's go."

"Where we going?"

"Lobstering."

They walked south along the beach. Chucho, cursing, struggled with the gasoline can for a while and then exchanged it for the duffel bag. Palm fronds waved sinuously in the wind, like undersea things, and the surf hummed and flashed. They walked two miles and then turned and started wading up a shallow freshwater creek that led into the mangrove swamp. The water came to mid-calf. The mud sucked at David's feet; with each step he had to pull his foot free and that released air bubbles which smelled like rotten eggs when they burst at the surface. Everything stank rottenly in here. It was like a sewer. And it was dark; David had to use his flashlight and insects flashed through the beam and whined around his ears. Chucho, half a dozen paces behind, was cursing and slapping at his body. Soft things lightly brushed David's face; insects, moss, leaves and vines—a bat?

The boat was floating in a shallow pool about three hundred yards into the swamp. The water was thickly covered with green scum and in the dim glow of the flashlight it looked like solid ground, a putting green or closely trimmed lawn. The old skiff was sixteen feet long, leaky and rotting now, the bottom covered with shellfish and moss. There was a six-horsepower Johnson outboard engine mounted on the transom, but it had been abused and left out in the sea air and was no longer reliable. He and Chucho usually stepped the mast and raised the patched, mildewed sail if the winds were light. Chucho had stolen the skiff from a village several miles down the coast.

The boat, half-filled with water (weeds and scum were beginning to grow on the inside now) was tethered to a tree. Chucho pulled the boat over to the bank and David shone his light on it.

Tadpoles were swimming around up in the bows. Clusters of gelatinous eggs floated on the water, and mosquito larvae rose to the surface and sank back again. The tiny, snorkled larvae, radiant worms in the flash-light beam, were jerkily rising and sinking throughout the length of the skiff—a partly comical, partly disgusting three-dimensional submarine ballet.

"Hey, man, look at that."

"It's a damned aquarium," David said.

"Aquarium yourself, man. Let's go rob the Nicholson place."

"No."

"This here boat ain't no good anymore."

"Help me empty it."

Moths were flicking against the flashlight and David's hand and arm. He placed the flashlight on a mangrove root, the beam angled toward the pool, and then he and Chucho hauled the skiff up onto dry land and tipped it over. Water, algae, tadpoles, eggs, and mosquito larvae spilled out. They righted the skiff then, pushed it back into the pool, and David threw his duffel bag inside and climbed in over the bow. The wood was slimy to his touch. His tennis shoes slipped on the scum.

Chucho passed across the gasoline can. "A great boat, huh, baby?"

"Come on, come on," David said. "The mosquitoes . . . "

Chucho retrieved the flashlight, pushed the boat away from the bank, and scrambled aboard.

"Oh, man, we should of gone to the Nicholson house. We're gonna drown, Flaco."

Several times the creek was too shallow or turned too sharply for the boat to pass, and then David jumped out and, knee-deep in water and muck, rocked and pushed it through.

He pulled the skiff through the final S turn and climbed back in over the transom. Ahead now, through the gnarled, mossy trees, he could see fireballs of surf and hear the crashing detonations.

At the estuary, they both had to get out and drag the skiff through the muddy tidal flats until it was again afloat. A big wave broke one hundred yards away; there were streaky flashes followed by a rim of tumbling foam and then the wave curled both ways from the center and thundered down.

The line of surf reached them and suddenly they were waist-deep in warm, boiling foam, and they nearly lost the boat. They climbed aboard, Chucho in the stern now, David in the center, and David began rowing hard. He had the backwash of the wave helping him for a time.

The next two combers were not much trouble but the third broke over the bow, spinning the skiff askew and nearly filling it. Chucho was on his knees, cursing and bailing with a two-liter coffee can. David kept rowing. It was like pulling upstream against a powerful current. Finally they were beyond the surf break-line. David's arms cramped from the strain but he continued rowing for another fifty yards before shipping the oars. The skiff rose lightly to the swells.

"We almost lost it that time, Jesus, my boy," he said.

Chucho dropped the coffee can and sat in the stern seat. "Hey, I don't swim."

"You tell me that every time we go out."

"What you got to drink tonight?"

"Rum."

"And Coca Cola."

"Right."

"Okay, Flaco, okay, get it out."

David unzipped the duffel bag and got out the rum and two bottles of Coke. Chucho bit off the caps, poured out a quarter of each bottle, and refilled them with rum.

"This ain't bad, Flaco."

"Put some gas in the motor and see if it'll start."

"We got gas from last time."

"Well, pull the cord."

Chucho pulled the starter cord several times but the engine would not fire. The skiff was drifting back toward the breaking surf.

"Take off the housing and clean the plugs," David said.

"Yessir, yessir, Captain."

David fitted the oars into the locks and rowed easily seaward, quartering into the swells. Each oar-stroke ignited a curving streak of phosphorescence in the water. The sea had a fishy plankton odor. The hills beyond the town were darkly silhouetted against the sky, black paper-cutout mountains, and pinpoints of light gleamed here and there—white for homes and streetlights, red and orange and blue for the commercial neons. David preferred to look seaward, toward the Orient, into the hissing sibilance of wind and sea.

The outboard motor stuttered and smoked, then died. Chucho pulled the starter cord again; it caught and ran roughly for a moment and then smoothed out.

"Ready, man?"

"Let's go."

"Here's a buoy, man." Chucho throttled the engine down to the idling speed and then shifted into neutral. An object thumped hollowly against the hull.

David lifted the big block of cork into the skiff and then began hauling up the lobster trap. He had forgotten his gloves tonight. The chain was covered with tiny barnacles and shellfish, and they cut his hands. He lifted the trap out of the water, let it drain for a moment, and then dropped it inside the skiff.

Chucho turned on the flashlight. "Five!"

Only once before had they ever found five lobsters in a single trap. David removed three of the lobsters—each with five-inch tails—and threw the trap, coil of chain and cork buoy overboard. They never took all of the lobsters, and they usually rebaited the trap with chunks of animal fat that David kept in a bottle in the duffel bag.

Chucho shifted the engine into forward and began hunting for another cork buoy.

They had a good night, twenty-four lobsters. They would keep four of the larger bugs for the ritual poacher's feast at David's room tomorrow and sell the remaining twenty to the Hotel Del Sol. The hotel paid two dollars for each lobster. They would split forty dollars then. David was living on the Mexican economy and twenty dollars did not seem bad for a few hours work. Of course, they were not always lucky enough to get so many lobsters. And it was not prudent to go poaching more than once a week.

They followed a big swell in toward the beach and after it broke, Chucho gunned the engine and they rode the tumbling surf all the way to the estuary. It took them thirty minutes to get the skiff back to the pool in the swamp, and when they returned to the beach it was beginning to get light.

"We could of stole a thousand dollars worth of stuff at Nicholsons' place," Chucho said.

"The sun's going to come up soon. Let's get away from here."

"You're a bully, man. You bully little kids like me and you choke the ladies."

"Cut that out!"

Chucho grinned. "Take it easy, take it easy, just kidding, man."

SIX

David dove a few feet, leveled off, and swam around the bulge of coral. Below, in shadows the color of laundry blueing, he saw a dozen good-sized fish. He finned downward. He could feel the pressure on his ears. About fifteen feet above the bottom he passed through the thermocline and for a moment the upper half of his body was in cold water while his legs trailed in the warmer water above.

There was a white sand arena enclosed on one side by the reef wall and elsewhere by tall sea plants. The fish he had selected was slowly swimming toward the fringe of weeds. It did not feel threatened; it was instinctually calculating his distance and angle and speed. But of course the fish did not know about spears.

David pumped hard and glided in. He led the fish, knowing that it would spurt forward when alarmed. He squeezed the trigger, the taut rubber band snapped free and the spear shaft streaked forward. The fish was impaled just in front of its gills; it flapped and struggled against the weight and barbs, and David could feel the vibrations through the length of the shaft. He coiled, turned, and began swimming up toward the bright, glazed surface. He was in need of air now. He pumped hard, passing the thermocline and on up through the water until finally breaking through the surface.

He blew water out of the snorkel and breathed deeply. He could taste salt. His hearing was dulled and there was a salty weight in his sinuses. The fish quivered stiffly on the end of his spear's shaft. He would eat well tonight, huachinango Veracruzano, the red snapper cooked with a spicy tomato sauce.

He heard a voice then and turned toward the beach. A girl in a bikini was standing on shore, waving at him. It was Maria Cristina Santistevan. He waved back and began swimming in.

Maria Cristina was beautiful, really beautiful, and bright, and haughty, and rebellious right up to the edge of losing her advantages. That is, she vaguely believed in a spontaneous, world-wide revolt after which everyone would have as much as she—the thought that she might then have less never occurred to her. She was a snob in a time of reverse snobbery and she tried to be ashamed of it. "God, David," she'd once said to him, "I want to love our poor Indians and mestizos. I would like to learn from them. Don't you believe that primitive peoples have a natural goodness and wisdom that could save our rotten Western civilization? I work hard at knowing and loving them, David, honestly I do. But then I look down and see their dusty, horny feet. I believe I *could* love them if they wore shoes." And then she tilted her head back and laughed, as she always did when surprising herself with the truth. Maria Cristina, David thought, probably *would* love the poor Indians and mestizos if they wore shoes. It was mostly a matter of aesthetics.

David left the fish in a small tidal pool and walked up through the sand. They embraced, separated, and then walked hand in hand up toward a palm where she had a blanket and a wicker picnic basket.

"You've gained weight," he said.

"Yes. Do you like it?"

"Absolutely."

"I've matured, haven't I?"

"You certainly have."

"I'm not sure I'm happy about it. I think I'd rather have remained a child. But you, David—you're so thin."

"I know."

"Poor baby. I have a picnic basket filled with good things. Cheese and bread and potato chips and oranges and papaya."

"Beer?"

"And beer, still cold."

They sat in the shade of the palm and she got out a bottle of beer and a Pepsi Cola and opened them.

"How long are you going to be home?"

"Two weeks, for the Easter holidays."

"Do you like going to school in the States?"

"It's all right. I don't like the cold and the snow very much."

"You've lost most of your accent. There's just a little sing-song left."

"Sing-song, is it? I speak English much better than you speak Spanish."

"Nearly everybody does."

"Are you hungry?"

"No." He sipped the beer, took one of her cigarettes, and lit it. "You're smoking now."

"I sneak them. Don't tell anyone."

"How did you know where I was?"

"I asked that evil little Aguilar boy."

"Does your father know you came to see me?"

"God, no! You know he doesn't approve of you. And now that you've taken to strangling girls . . . "

"I'm getting awfully tired of that stuff. So your father won't permit you to see me."

"I'm seeing you now. But we can't meet publicly." She leaned forward and kissed him lightly on the cheek, straightened, and said, "Could you tell? I'm not a virgin anymore."

"Aren't you?"

"I met this really handsome—"

"I don't want to hear about it."

She smiled. "Jealous, baby?"

"Yes."

"Really?"

"I said yes."

"Don't get mad. I was only teasing. I'm still a virgin, but only barely. I may be the only nineteen-year-old virgin left. There really was a man—a professor at college—and we were undressed in his apartment and everything, but then he was impotent. He said it had never happened before. I'll bet he tells that to all the girls."

"I told you that I didn't want to hear about it."

"He said that he was intimidated by my exquisite beauty. He said that it would be like violating a Madonna. Wasn't that sweet?"

"I see you're learning to be bitchy, Maria Cristina."

"Are you going to deflower me soon?"

"Sure," he said. "Right now is fine."

"No, not here."

"Where?"

"Maybe I'll select Felix Mondragon for the defloration."

"Really bitchy."

"Is it true that you're going to play Felix in a tennis match?"

"Maybe," David said. "Harry Rudd and your father are trying to arrange it."

"He'll beat you, David."

"Will he?"

"Oh, yes, certainly."

"Why are you so sure?"

"Because Felix is very, very good."

"And I'm not?"

"You're good, David, but not that good."

"Maybe we'll find out how good I am."

"I don't want to see you humiliated."

"Thank you."

"Felix was on our Davis Cup team."

"Oh, well, I'll concede the match then."

"David, stop being so stubborn and intense. You used to be so much fun."

"That was in the days before I developed an appetite for choking and raping girls, and then throwing them over cliffs."

She laughed.

"Do you like Mondragon?" he asked her.

"Felix is a very nice boy."

"Felix is a hotdog."

"You must be getting hungry. Are you?"

They ate lunch, swam for half an hour and then Maria Cristina returned to the village.

He and Maria Cristina had been close friends the previous summer before she had gone off to school, excruciatingly chaste lovers (she'd been only eighteen then, and not ready), and David had vaguely thought about marriage someday, when she had matured, when he'd managed to order his chaotic life. But they both had changed in eight months, Maria Cristina especially. And now he wasn't sure he would be able to break through her vast, careless narcissism.

SEVEN

David sat at an outdoor café on the small town plaza, sipping a glass of Peñafiel mineral water and watching the townspeople and tourists walk by. Shoe-shine boys and newspaper boys and beggars and blind lottery-ticket salesmen—led by solemn, protective children—circulated among the tables. David had his shoes shined, and bought three of the blue lottery tickets. Rich by Saturday, who knows?

Maria Cristina came striding down the sidewalk, her heels clicking on the pavement, her tanned legs and arms bare, her hair ignited by the sun. Erotic in an ordinary sundress. Young, imperious, special. Everyone in the café and along the street turned to look at her.

She saw David and hesitated (he began to rise from his chair), and then she narrowed her eyes, smiling with them alone, formed her mouth into a brief kiss, regained the rhythm of her walk, and went on. She went out of sight then and all of the men on the terrace stared avidly at the space she had vacated.

David sat down. She could not be seen with him in public. He could understand that. No, he couldn't.

A few minutes later he saw Captain Vigil coming toward him. He was wearing a shot-silk suit and as he weaved in and out of the tables, the sunlight struck shimmering rainbows on the fabric. He nodded brusquely, pulled out the chair across from David, and sat down.

"I've received a report on you from the FBI," he said.

"Oh, Christ," David said.

"Does that disturb you?"

"Of course it does. Are you going to send me back to the States?"

"What would happen if I did?"

"You must know."

"I am asking."

David hesitated. "No, you tell me."

"Do you think I am bluffing?"

"I don't know."

"Two felonies—introducing prohibited substances into the U.S., and unlawful flight to avoid prosecution."

"Well . . . "

"So then, what would happen to you if I sent you back?"

"I'd probably go to jail."

"Yes. For long, do you think?"

"One day in jail is too long."

"Agreed." Vigil half turned in his chair, raised a hand, and when the waiter arrived he ordered two more bottles of the mineral water. He smiled at David. He was not an ugly man until he smiled.

"So," he said. "Drugs, eh?"

"That sounds . . . "

"Dirty?"

"Are you interested in hearing about it?"

"Why not?"

"It was only grass, one run. I was trying to get a good stake so that I could concentrate on pro tennis for a couple of years. I didn't see myself as being more criminal than the men who ran booze into the coast during Prohibition."

"Please, your rationalizations do not concern me; they are personal."

David shrugged. "I got caught."

"And then jumped bail and ran. Unlawful flight to avoid prosecution."

"That's right."

"A fatuous charge. It seems unfair somehow to put a man in jail because of his very reasonable efforts to stay out of jail. What happened to your hand?"

"What?"

Vigil gestured. "There."

David looked down at the small cuts around the knuckles of his right hand. "I cut it on coral yesterday."

"Yes? I would expect that coral cuts would be on the palms, from pulling oneself along."

David turned his hands palms-up to show the cuts there.

The waiter brought two bottles of mineral water, two glasses, and a plate containing sliced limes.

Vigil filled his glass. "The girl was very badly beaten that night, before she was strangled. Two teeth were broken. It seems likely that the killer received cuts on his knuckles."

"Wait, hey, wait, Vigil, these are fresh cuts."

Vigil smiled faintly and nodded.

"You know damned well that I didn't have any cuts on my hands the day after the murder."

"Please, don't get excited. People are staring at you." He sipped his water, took a lime from the plate, and squeezed it into the glass. "It's true, those cuts are fresh, and you didn't have any cuts the day I saw you."

David slowly exhaled. "Why do you want to frighten me this way?"

Vigil shrugged, lit a cigarette.

David helped himself to a cigarette from the policeman's package. Raleighs—for some odd reason a prestige cigarette in Mexico.

"I didn't know it had been that brutal," David said.

"Of course it was brutal. Murder is brutal. It's brutal psychologically, philosophically, and it is always brutal physically. There is blood, pain, terror. And this kind of murder, a sex murder, is the most brutal of all."

"Listen, Vigil, you don't—"

"Why don't you call me Captain or Señor Vigil? Is not my position worthy of some respect?"

"I'm sorry. But you don't really believe that I killed the girl, do you?"

"You Americans, all of you, are so strange to me that I cannot tell when I sit down face-to-face with one if he is a model citizen of your republic or a liar and murderer. I know your language, I've lived among you, and I still can't evaluate you as I can my countrymen."

"You could ask the people who know me well."

"I have. Doctor Pacheco speaks well of you."

"He speaks ill of me to my face."

"It's odd—the Mexicans speak well of you. But the Americans seem to have serious reservations. Many of your American friends and acquaintances have been tentative about endorsing your character."

"Who?"

"I can't tell you that, of course. But remember what said about myself being unable to clearly understand Americans? Well, shouldn't your countrymen be more sensitive to your psychology than a Mexican, even one as intelligent and perceptive as Dr. Pacheco? Or as lovely as Maria Cristina Santistevan? I don't know."

"How can I defend myself against these vague rumors, this malice?" David said angrily. "What the hell are you doing, relying on your woman's intuition?"

Vigil held up a forefinger. "And I must consider your previous troubles with the police and courts in the U.S."

"I told you about that. It was just the one time."

"Once that has been recorded. But how many offenses have you committed without being arrested or charged?"

"None!"

"So you say."

"In my entire life I got into trouble once, for a trivial crime."

"The statutes of the State of Florida do not believe that it was so trivial. The U.S. Justice Department does not believe that flight to avoid prosecution is trivial."

"You yourself said that that was a fatuous charge."

"And so it is. Listen, I am saying that you have been in trouble in the past and are presently a fugitive. Eighty percent of the serious crime is committed by five percent of the population. Persons who have been arrested for felony crime in the past will very likely be arrested in the future. Do you see? If there has been a sex offense I will immediately question all sex offenders who are known to me. I don't care if one has been clean for twenty years—I shall want to talk to that man. Isn't that logical? If there has been a burglary I will—"

"But we're talking about murder!"

"And in murder I will be most interested in the suspect who has a criminal record. Listen, most citizens will cheat on their tax, offer or accept an illegal gratuity, leave the scene of an accident, steal objects from their workplace, buy stolen merchandise, assault someone in a bar—I have no illusions about the virtue of the good, solid, ordinary citizen, the backbone of every society. Ah, but you see, there is a difficult barrier to cross for most, a vast step—to commit a serious felony. Armed robbery. Strong-armed robbery. Kidnapping. Perhaps even smuggling. You have crossed that barrier. Murder then becomes only a matter of degree, an escalation. The barrier is down."

"Look, this is crazy. I did something greedy and stupid. I've paid for it and I'm still paying. My whole future is in doubt because of something that I regarded at the time as little more than a prank."

"A potentially very profitable prank."

"But, my God, to say that because I tried to smuggle a few bales of marijuana into the States that I automatically became capable of murdering that poor, miserable, lost girl . . . Look, I'll take a polygraph test."

Vigil shook his head. "We don't often use the polygraph in this country. Do you know why? Most of our people don't even know what they are. Not understanding, they don't believe. Not believing, the results are usually inconclusive. The polygraph is similar to sorcery—one must believe in it before it is effective. Anyway, as you probably know, your own courts will not admit the results of a polygraph test into evidence."

"Well, what the hell can I do?"

"Wait."

"Have you talked to my landlady, the people who live on the street?"

"Yes. They corroborate your story. The girl was heard desperately shouting and weeping late in the evening."

"It wasn't late!"

"It seemed late to your neighbors, people who rise at dawn."

"And did they tell you that she left alone?"

"Yes. She was in the street at around ten, alone, and she went away."

David leaned back in his chair and slowly exhaled.

The policeman sipped his mineral water.

"Then you know that much, at least," David said.

"I know that she left your room at ten o'clock and that you did not *immediately* follow her. I also know that the young woman caused a remarkable disturbance and left in anger and sadness."

Vigil stood up. "It's pleasant here. I wish I could stay." He reached into his trouser pocket and withdrew some folded currency.

"I've got the check," David said.

"Thank you. I only drank half of my water. Why don't you finish the bottle?"

"Okay. When I'm finished do you want me to throw the glass against the wall?"

Vigil stared intently at him and then said, "Still flippant, are you, my friend? All toasty warm and secure in the shelter of the U.S. Constitution and the Bill of Rights?" He unbuttoned his suit jacket, reached inside, withdrew a pair of handcuffs and very swiftly locked one end around David's wrist, pulled the chain taut, and snapped the other ring closed on the table's awning pole.

"What the hell . . . "

Vigil showed his mad-dog grin.

"This is ridiculous," David said. He glanced around the terrace; people at the other tables were smiling at him, and a few watchers had gathered on the sidewalk.

Vigil leaned over the table, his face close, and very quietly said, "It is necessary that you sit down for a time and consider your difficult situation. Perhaps you will decide to tell me the truth. You see, I am convinced that you murdered that girl, and I intend to see that you are punished for it. You have been viewing the matter altogether too lightly and—"

"No, I'm not."

"—and I do not appreciate that."

"What do you want me to do? Cry? Beg? Crawl?"

"I want you to realize that I possess a great deal of power and you have none. For example, I can handcuff you to this table, humiliate you in public, cause you physical and mental discomfort. And that, *señor*, is an extremely modest example of my power."

"This is absurd."

Vigil showed his mirthless, snaggle-toothed grin once more, turned, and left the café.

David was chained to the table for almost nine hours. At first he almost enjoyed his predicament; he joked with the patrons, called to passing acquaintances to join him for a drink, ordered a light lunch which he ate left-handed, borrowed a newspaper and read it. But then he became annoyed by the stares, the animal-in-a-zoo aspect. His humiliation and rage gradually increased. Vigil—how he hated that man.

At three o'clock the café was empty and there were only a few persons on the street. He called out to the waiters who concealed him with tablecloths while he urinated into a bucket.

Later he lowered his head onto his left forearm and dozed lightly. He was not protected from the sun now; its heavy light slanted in beneath the awning and he was drenched with sweat, sickened by the pulsing heat. There was no breeze. His table had not been cleared and flies walked over the plates and glasses.

After five o'clock people returned to the streets and by six the café was nearly full. He had become a kind of pariah now; friends spoke to him briefly, attempted jokes, but he could see that they were embarrassed, and contemptuous. A party of American residents came in for dinner and pointedly did not look at him or speak. Irrationally, he began to feel guilty. *He* knew that he had not harmed the girl, but these others didn't, and so he started to feel vaguely guilty of the crime. Strange, he thought; it seemed that punishment triggered guilt instead of the other way around.

He wanted to hide and could not. There was no escaping these eyes, the weight of disapproval, of hatred even.

He saw now the intent and efficacy of the old-time stocks, the calculated brutality, the *social* aspect.

The neons and street lights came on. A line formed at the box office of the movie theater across the street. He ordered a ham and cheese sandwich but could not finish it.

At nine o'clock two grinning, uniformed policemen came onto the terrace and released him. His right arm was numb from fingertips to shoulder.

He slowly walked home down the back streets, thinking that Vigil had been right about one thing. Fear. David had never really been frightened until now; he confused anxiety with fear. Vigil had made his point about fear and power. The man could do just about anything he wanted to do.

EIGHT

David looked over the net and concentrated on one of the three tennis ball cans he had set up in the opposite court. This one, the only still standing, was at the right-angle juncture of the service court endline and the sideline. Sunlight glinted off the dented yellow cylinder. The can seemed to quiver, to jump three-dimensionally out of a flat background. His concentration was superb this morning; it had gone beyond a deliberate, conscious focus into that semi-hypnotic state when it seems that a distant object has become an extension of the self.

He bounced the tennis ball three times with his racket, paused, coiled, tossed the ball up and began uncoiling, cocked his arm, and whipped the racket overhead. He felt the shock on his wrist and forearm. The ball streaked over the net, hit the can at its base, and sent it in a high, spinning arc. Three in a row. A good time to quit for the day.

David had been practicing on Harry Rudd's court for a week, and he had played two matches with the teaching professional at the Golf and Tennis Club and had won easily. The match with Mondragon was scheduled for Saturday morning. He intended to avoid tennis on Friday, not even think about it, and so he had only two more days of preparation.

David was confident, believed that he would win the match, but it might be close. He had the power serve, the net game. Mondragon had the ground strokes. Mondragon was probably in better physical condition but he was not accustomed to the humid coastal heat, as David was. About even so far. But then Aurelio Santistevan, a Mondragon partisan, had insisted that the match be played on his own "neutral" court, somehow thinking that this would favor his boy. Harry Rudd, knowing that the hard-surfaced court favored the player with the power game, David, had hypocritically argued with Aurelio about the site of the match, slowly weakened, and then finally submitted on the condition that the party Saturday night would be held at his "neutral" home.

An ordinary tennis match had been turned into a duel with nationalistic overtones. The Mexicans were rooting for and betting on Felix Mondragon. The American colony had been maneuvered into backing David. They were not enthusiastic.

David left the court, walked down a little grassy hill and entered the patio-swimming pool area. There had been a strong wind last night and petals from the bougainvillea and jasmine and jacaranda floated on amethyst-colored water. Harry's two Doberman pinschers—Rasputin and Torquemada—were sleeping in the sun. They raised their narrow, reptilian heads to gaze at him, sniffed the air, then lay back again. Spooky, paranoid animals, aptly named.

David lit a cigarette (he had cut down to five cigarettes a day until after the match) and looked up at the high dive. He decided not to go off the platform today. The pool looked the size of a playing card from up there, and you had to enter the water just right or there was a danger of striking bottom. Harry called the high dive his "Towel of Babel." He liked to say that if he hadn't stopped the Mexican workmen they would have built it clear into heaven. Harry blamed the Mexicans but it was really his own fault; he had designed it himself in foot measurements, forgetting that Mexico used the metric system, and so instead of being ten feet high the platform was thirty feet above the pool apron. David was the only one who ever used it.

The screen door slammed and Harry came down the steps and toward him. "How's the training going, kid?" he asked. His voice was husky. His thinning, sandy hair was rumpled, there were sleep-creases on his cheek, and his eyes were red and puffy.

"Morning, Harry."

"Do you want to rally some?"

"No, not this morning."

"Thank God."

"You're trembling, Harry."

"Jesus Christ. Jesus."

"You should have left some in the bottom of the jug."

"Jesus. Let's get out of the sun."

They went down to the terrace and sat beneath an umbrellaed table.

"Guadalupe is brewing coffee. Do you want some?"

"Sure."

"Breakfast?"

"Sounds fine."

"Listen, do you still think you can beat Mondragon? If not, you can sprain an ankle or something."

"I'm pretty sure that I'll win."

"I've got a lot of money riding on you, Dave Daiquiri."

"How much?"

"About nine hundred dollars so far."

"I'm sorry I asked."

"Every goddamned Mexican in town wants to bet me. I took a fifty-peso bet from Manuel yesterday."

"What kind of odds are you getting?"

"Some four to one, but mostly three to one."

"Well, Harry, I'm confident that I'm going to beat him but it isn't a cinch, you know."

Rudd sighed and rubbed his eyes. "I know. I stopped betting on you three days ago and started betting on the flag."

"Don't take any more bets."

"I'll probably have to. My manhood has somehow become involved. These Mexicans turn everything into a test of masculinity. They think with their balls. *Huevos* this, *cojones* that."

The servant placed a bottle of cognac on the table, served them coffee, and took David's order for breakfast.

Harry, his hand trembling, poured an ounce of cognac into his coffee.

"You've been hitting the sauce pretty hard lately haven't you, Harry?" David said.

"Yeah, well . . . I don't know. Norma's still in the States. She generally keeps me in line. And I've got so much loose time on my hands. I worked my ass off for twenty-five years, kid, built up the second-largest GM dealership in the Midwest, retired to the sun to enjoy myself. Leisure is highly overrated, remember that."

"Well, I've never seen you go overboard with the booze. Take it easy."

"No sermons, absolutely-no-sermons-this-morning."

"Okay."

"Or any other morning, now that I think about it."

"Did you talk to Vigil about me, Harry?"

"Yeah. I did what I could for you. I lied like hell. I only wanted to make you an Eagle Scout but I got inspired and now you're a candidate for sainthood. 'Would you say that David Rhodes has a violent temper?' 'No, sir, butter wouldn't melt in that chap's mouth.' 'To your knowledge, does Mr. Rhodes take drugs, or alcohol to excess?' 'Oh, no, sir, a clean-living lad.' 'Would you say that Rhodes was sexually impulsive?' 'Captain, sir, that I cannot answer for I am married and faithful to my wife's gender.'"

"Well, I hope you did me some good. Some of the Americans here gave Vigil the thumbs-down on me."

"Yeah? Who?"

"I don't know, Vigil wouldn't say. He's a strange cop—running around collecting character references on a murder suspect."

"It makes sense. He's got to be careful."

"The strain is getting to me. I'm obviously his number-one suspect, the only one probably, and I just never know what's going to happen."

"Have you thought about scooting back to the States?"

"I've considered it. No, Vigil would love to see me run."

"Look, Dave, everything will turn out fine. Don't get all tight and anxious about it. At least not until after the tennis match."

"Did Vigil tell you anything?"

"Tell me anything?"

"About the case."

"He said that they haven't got an identity on the girl yet. But that could be baloney. It might be that he's trying to keep the whole thing as quiet as possible until after the Easter tourist influx has exfluxed."

"Maybe he'll arrest me after the holidays."

"Here comes your breakfast—enough to make a python vomit."

"Did Vigil say anything else?"

"He stated Mondragon would beat you and backed that conjecture with a five-hundred-peso wager."

NINE

Temporary wooden bleachers with dried palm-frond roofs had been erected on the hillside above Aurelio Santistevan's tennis court. It was nearly ten o'clock now and the bleachers were filled. The crowd's bright clothing was a shifting kaleidoscopic blur of color against the green of the hill, and their talk and laughter sounded to David like the noises in an aviary. Servants carried trays of coffee, orange and grapefruit juice, and breakfast rolls. Small children shrieked and ran. There were too many people here who did not know anything about tennis. It was a party.

Felix Mondragon had not taken the warm-up seriously; he'd seemed bored in a lazy, cheerful way, and made David look awkward with a couple of topspin lobs. David suppressed his irritation. He worked on his timing and concentration, tried to shut out Mondragon and the crowd. He had to achieve the psychological equivalent of tunnel vision.

Mondragon left the court and David was alone for a moment and then he saw Harry Rudd swaggering toward him. Harry was gnawing on a big cigar. He wore sandals, plaid Bermuda shorts, a tank shirt, and a cap with a green celluloid visor. His arms and legs were hairy; his moves aggressive. Rudd liked to make a bad impression on those whom he considered to be enemies, and he did not mind turning himself into a parody in order to do so.

He stopped close enough so that David could smell his cigar breath and aftershave lotion. "Kid," he said, "it's tough dealing with these totalitarians."

"What's the trouble?"

"They insist you wear your shirt for the match."

"Why?"

"I don't know. Harassment. Propriety."

"It's got to be ninety degrees already, and the humidity can't be much lower than that."

"I know. But listen, concede this point and it gives me leverage on getting Peralta to be head judge. I've been arguing for Grimes but I really don't want him. Peralta's a Mexican and on the other side, but he's basically square. I want him. I don't want Grimes and I especially don't want Garcia."

"Harry . . . "

"I know, kid, politics right up to the gun, but that's the world. You don't have to worry about it. Let me worry. Okay?"

"I'll wear the shirt."

Rudd patted him on the arm. "Relax. Look, I got a whole pharmacy over at our bench. If you want a ben or something later, let me know and I'll slip it into your orange juice."

"Just orange juice, Harry. Lots of it and not too cold."

"You okay, Dave Daiquiri?"

"Yeah. Listen, whoever you get for umpire, tell him to keep those children quiet."

"Sure. Anything else?"

"Just keep an eye on things, details. Make sure I get fresh tennis balls when I'm due. Keep track of the score yourself, don't rely on the officials. Keep alert, you're defending my interests."

"I'm defending *my* interests."

David walked over to the bench and sat down. Next to the bench was the scorer's table, and on the other side, the Mondragon bench. David removed his shoes, smoothed out the wrinkles in his socks, pulled on his shoes, and laced them. Too tight. He tried again. Too loose. He could hear Harry arguing with Aurelio Santistevan; both men wanted Peralta for head judge but each was reluctant to mention him. Peralta was the compromise and it was not yet time for that. David laced his shoes again and they felt just right.

". . . let's call it off," Harry was saying.

Aurelio: "Well, we could try Peralta."

"I respect Juan, but . . . "

"I agree then, let's call it off."

"Okay, okay, shit, I give up, I'll accept Peralta."

Mondragon was out on the court now, standing by the net. David got up and walked out there and they shook hands. "*Mucha suerte,*" Mondragon said. "*Suerte,* Felix," David said, and he turned and walked back to the baseline of the court he was defending. He was floating with the trembly lightness that came when adrenaline was pumping. He was buoyant. The anxieties of the past two years vanished and he was left purified. It was so good to again be facing an opponent who could be seen and defeated. Here, in a couple of hours, something would be resolved. That sliver of time would have a clearly defined beginning, middle and end, and though reliant on time, it somehow seemed independent of time. He would beat Mondragon if he played very well. He would lose if he played poorly. How clean that concept was. There was order; it was all measured and symmetrical and the sequence did not vary. You could make a mistake but you could not be wrong. The grays, the doubts, the ambiguities were all fenced out.

David felt that sometimes he used the tools available—space and time, a ball, a racket, his body—and made something extraordinary out of them, became, for isolated moments, an artist.

"Service!" Judge Peralta called from the tower.

David went into a semi-crouch and began swaying gently from side to side. Something inside of him was coiling. It hurt. He could barely breathe. A familiar physical clock began keeping time in microseconds.

The tennis ball, cleanly white against the green background, had separated from Mondragon and was rising, and Mondragon uncoiled, seeming to grow very tall, and the ball streaked over the net.

"Fault!" the service line judge called.

David's tension evaporated and for a moment he was tired. He was now ready to play tennis.

The first game went to deuce before Mondragon won it. David took the second game, Mondragon the third, David the fourth, each holding service, but then Felix won the next four games. They were all very close. David had lost the first set 2-6. He was sorry that as long as he had lost the set he hadn't forced Mondragon to work harder in this heat and humidity; 6-7 or 4-6 would have been better.

Harry Rudd looked at him as Christ must have looked at Judas; Caesar at Brutus.

David toweled his face and arms and drank half a glass of orange juice with two salt tablets.

"Settle down," Rudd said.

"Relax, Harry. This is the best of five sets match."

"Yeah, and at this rate it'll be over by eleven thirty."

David walked out onto the court. His shirt was already soaked through with sweat; he felt as though he had a fever. In another half hour the sun would be murderous; he hoped it would kill Mondragon first.

It was Mondragon's serve. He was very loose and confident now, swinging freely, and he hit some beautiful shots to win the first game of the second set.

David served. It felt good and he knew it was an ace before it cleared the net. He double-faulted twice in a row then, but all four serves were powerfully hit and just barely outside the lines. He served a slice that pulled Mondragon wide and then volleyed away the return. It was coming. He could feel it coming now. He double-faulted again. Don't panic, for Christ's sake, keep ripping the ball, don't start aiming.

He shrugged to relax his shoulder muscles. He inhaled, held the breath, slowly exhaled. Then he tossed up the ball, unwound, rising and swinging, hit it hard and flat down the center line.

"Fault!"

What? What! Some members of the crowd were whistling the call. Harry Rudd was on his feet, screaming, "Didn't you see that, didn't you watch the ball, you goddamned blind dizzy son of a bitch!" The entire crowd began whistling then, a low harmonic whistle that gradually rose in volume and pitch until it hurt David's ears. Christ, he knew it, those people were acting like this was a bullfight. Harry was no better—this isn't a baseball game, Harry.

The crowd was still whistling when David hit his second serve. He double-faulted again and was now down two games in the set. Mondragon was really cocky now, posing and clowning like a detestable sort of Cantinflas.

David was rattled and his ground strokes began to go to pieces; he missed shots that Maria Cristina could have returned without effort. He was now down 0-3 in the second set. What was happening?

He pretended that there was a stone in his shoe. He limped back and forth along the baseline (a few members of the crowd began whistling the unauthorized delay), and then he sat down and unlaced his shoe. He removed his shoe and shook out an invisible pebble. Not concentrating, he thought. Worried about the officials, Harry, the crowd. Seeing just about everything except the tennis ball, watching Mondragon's antics, glancing up at Maria Cristina sitting on the grass next to the bleachers. Thinking but not concentrating.

Peralta was ordering play to resume. Was that the second warning?

David very slowly laced up his shoe, his hands trembling with humiliation and rage. Three shots, three good shots in a row and he would be on his way back. Let it out, go for it, swing hard and free. Stop thinking, let the body alone to do what it knows how to do. Encourage the dream man.

David served another ace, his fifth of the match. Mondragon returned the next serve into the net. He blooped the next serve back and David put away the volley. The dream man is coming. Felix won the next point with a fine backhand passing shot, and then David came back with another service ace. Six. How do you like that serve, punk?

He broke Mondragon's service, then they each held serve until the score was 6-6. Mondragon was the tiebreaker. There had been several poor calls, and Mondragon had lucked out on several shots—one off the wood and two net-corders—but David knew he was going to win.

He felt stronger, more confident with every point. Mondragon had lost his edge. Felix, you're beginning to wilt, son. You and me are the only ones here who suspect that you are losing.

David sat down on the bench and sipped orange juice.

"God," Harry said. "We almost had him."

"Don't talk, Harry."

"Goddamn it, more bad calls."

"Please shut up, Harry."

"But you're starting to come back. It isn't over yet. Look at Mondragon—the guy looks like a refugee from hell. He's already lost ten pounds. Listen, if you—"

David got up and returned to the court. Shut up, Harry, just shut your big mouth.

David won the third set 6-2. He could do nothing wrong, everything worked. He had been drained of self-awareness and then refilled with magic. He was better than he had any right to be; he was whole, one complete thing, and even the linesmen seemed to realize it for they started granting him the questionable calls. And he had luck. It was all over, but only he and Felix knew it.

David won the first game of the fourth set and then he became aware of his exhaustion. His strokes lost some of their smoothness and force and accuracy. But it didn't matter now; Felix was beaten. David won the second and third games of the set and during the fourth, Mondragon stupidly dived for a ball that was already past him, and when he arose he was grimacing and holding his right shoulder.

"No," David said.

Mondragon looked at him, shook his head and slowly walked off the court.

Harry approached. "We've won, kid."

"He's going to quit on me," David said bitterly.

"Listen, he's got five minutes. That's the rule we agreed on in case of an injury. If he's not back out here in five minutes, he forfeits."

"I don't want a forfeit. I want to beat him on the court."

"Use your head, David Daiquiri. Take a win any way you can."

"No. I've got him now. Don't you see? There's nothing wrong with his shoulder, he's faking. Give him more than the five minutes. Give him as much time as he wants. When he gets a little rest he might—"

"Are you crazy? Listen, David, I've got a lot of money riding on this match."

"I've got more than money riding on it. I want a clean win, Harry. I need it."

"You're just not doing that good. You're down two sets to one."

"And I'm ahead in this set three-zip, and forty-fifteen, I've won seven games in a row. And I'm ahead in total games seventeen to fifteen."

"Yeah, okay, I can see it now. You're beating him."

"Harry, Jesus, man, listen, he's quitting now because he knows I've got him. That's the way he is. He's folded. But he's still technically ahead two sets to one. Everyone will say that he was beating me when he was injured."

"I don't care what they say as long as they pay their debts."

"Harry, I understand. You have a lot of money bet on this match. But listen—he's finished for today. He quit. He might beat me tomorrow. But not today, Harry, I've broken him for today; he can't, he cannot come back and win this match. So let me win, Harry."

Rudd looked at his watch. "He's got three more minutes."

David turned and left the court. Mondragon's shirt had been removed and one of Aurelio Santistevan's lackeys was rubbing his shoulder with oil. David moved close and could smell wintergreen and sweat.

"Felix," he said. "Listen, man, take as long as you need."

Mondragon looked up at him. His eyes were dull; his mouth was twisted downward.

"Take half an hour if you want. I'll wait. Okay?"

Aurelio cleared his throat. "Your patron and I have established certain rules."

"Rudd isn't my patron," David said. "And to hell with the rules. We're the athletes, we'll decide."

"Two minutes," Rudd called.

"Felix?" David said.

"I don't know . . . "

"Hey, come on, we'll go out and hit for a few minutes and you can judge how your shoulder feels."

"My shoulder . . . " Mondragon said. "No, no, I don't think I can do it."

"Is that the same shoulder that got hurt when you played the Fonseca kid last year? When you had to retire?"

Mondragon saw the contempt in David's eyes, heard it in his voice and turned away.

"Just about time," Harry Rudd said.

David went to his bench and sheathed his racket. "It's over," he said.

Rudd offered his hand but David pretended not to see it.

"I'm going," he said.

"Aren't you staying for lunch? Aurelio's put on a fine spread."

"No, I'm going."

"Well, okay, I'll give you a ride into town and then come back here. Goddamn, Dave, we beat them."

"We know that."

Harry slapped him roughly on the shoulder. "You are the official winner of this tennis match."

"Don't touch me," he said. And then, not wanting to be mean to Rudd: "A win is a win."

"You bet. You're coming to my party tonight, aren't you?"

"Sure, I'll be there."

"Are you still mad at me?"

"Yes, Harry, a little."

"That's because you're still heated up and competitive. Come on. Got any booze at your place?"

"Some rum."

"Rum, hell! We'll stop at my place for a second, lad, and pick up a couple bottles of champagne. Okay? Sure."

TEN

The night was hot and soft and reeked of flowers. The ladies' perfumes smelled cheap and artificial in comparison to the scents of real jasmine and lilac and rose. Chinese lanterns in the primary colors were strung around the pool and terrace areas, and other tiny red and blue and yellow paper lanterns glowed in the highest branches of the frangipani and hibiscus trees. Blossoms drifted on the swimming pool. The pool was a deep, glowing emerald which reflected the colored lights and shivered in the gusts of hot wind.

There were two musical groups, local mariachis and a quintet from Veracruz that played bastard Caribbean rhythms. Guests were dancing on the terrace. Servants carried platters of drinks and *antejitos* through the crowd. Inside the house there was a long table filled with food: salads, desserts, shrimp steamed in beer, oysters in the half shell, smoked fish and marinated fish, butter clams, caviar, cold lobster tail, a huge smoke-cured ham, quail and duck and dove, a roast kid, tongue, liver pâté, even iguana—it was a spread that made David's most gluttonous food dreams appear ascetic. He was hungry now but he intended to wait until his hunger became nearly unbearable, until saliva filled his mouth and his stomach cramped, before surrendering. The way to enjoy this kind of meal was to suffer for several hours and then, in the ensuing hours, gradually relieve the suffering. Hadn't Freud said that pleasure was the release of tension?

There was a large bar inside the house and a smaller portable bar down by the shallow end of the swimming pool. David was drinking champagne again, Mumm's— Harry Rudd did not cut corners when he gave a party. This one would take most of his winnings. David thought it was a fine party, just fine. He was a little drunk and he felt like a character in a book or movie, Nick Carroway or the young Prince Andre, or maybe Bogart in one of his white dinner jacket roles.

David wandered happily among the crowd.

"How're you feeling, kid?" Harry Rudd asked.

"Fine, kid," David said.

"Go easy on that champagne. It goes down smooth but it can tear off the top of your head."

"I'm fine, Harold."

"Sure, I know. Have a good time."

"Will do, kid."

Harry gave him a slantwise look and shook his head.

"Run along now, kid," David said. "Enjoy."

Nancy Cole asked him how his book of poetry was progressing.

"Splendidly," David said. "Superbly."

"When will your book be finished, David?"

"Soon, Mrs. Cole. Yes, quite right, soon."

"I know that it will be a beautiful book, David. Because you are a beautiful, beautiful person. Don't object, it's true, you really are. I never believed for one blink that you murdered that young girl." Mrs. Cole was drunk too.

"Thank you so much. Splendid."

"I really am so anxious to read your poems."

David occasionally wrote light verse with which to amuse Dr. Pacheco. Paco called him the Nightingale of Philistia.

"Ah, well, Mrs. Cole," David said. "I could recite one or two."

"I'd love it."

"There is one called 'Farewell to a Third Grade Chum.'"

"Yes?"

"But you wouldn't care to hear it."

"But I would, David, you awful tease."

"It goes like this. 'Oh pneumonia, inflamed tissues, cadenced rattles, phlegmy issues, no more tattles, good-bye, chum.'"

Mrs. Cole was embarrassed for him. She smiled nervously. "Oh, that's very nice."

Doctor Francisco Pacheco was gaudily attired in white shoes and trousers, a red blazer, a rose-colored ruffled shirt, and a red ascot with white polka dots.

"Hello, dummy," Pacheco said.

"You look like a fag fire plug, Paco."

"You look like the ticket taker in a Milwaukee movie theater, dummy."

"Call me dummy once more and I'll throw you and your gorgeous costume into the swimming pool."

"I'm drip-dry, punk. The costume is wash-and-wear. What did you say to Nancy Cole to make her run away from you like that?"

"Ah, yes, I recited one of my splendid poems."

Pacheco laughed. "Stop, stop, please."

David repeated the verse.

Pacheco shook his head. "There it is again, I constantly overestimate you."

"What are you doing here, Paco? I thought Harry Rudd disliked you."

"If Harry invited only the people he liked the place would be deserted except for Harry. And maybe you, crud."

"Call me crud once more and I'll break your tiny legs."

"Harry does like you. Maybe because you earn him money. The crumb won one hundred dollars from me this morning on the tennis match."

"You should have bet on me."

"I know."

"Aren't you going to tell me that Mondragon would have won if he hadn't gotten hurt?"

"No."

"I'm surprised."

"I had no idea you were that good."

"No one did."

"I know, I know. Except you and Rudd."

"Harry didn't know, really. He was just taking my word for it."

"You two took the entire town. Bastards. And that Mondragon—maybe he was in on it."

"No."

"Look at him over there, posing like a Greek statue. If I ever get him into surgery I'll cut off his vestigial balls. I'll cut out his heart if I can find it. Look at him. And look at that luscious Maria Cristina—Christ, I think that little baby is coming into estrus."

"You're really foul, Paco."

"Go away. One hundred dollars. If Norma Rudd were here I'd try to seduce her. Maybe I can steal some of the silver. One hundred dollars. Got any idea how many sutures that is? How many babies crapping on your trousers?"

"See you, Paco."

"Good-bye, chum," Dr. Pacheco said, laughing.

Maria Cristina's father gravely shook hands with David. "Good evening, David," he said.

"Good evening, Don Aurelio."

"You played well today."

"Thank you."

"It was unfortunate that the match was not completed."

"Yes."

"Did you know that Felix was on our Davis Cup team several years ago?"

"I knew that, yes."

"He is a very fine young man. I've known his mother and father for years. He comes of a very good family. An old family, good breeding."

David danced with Maria Cristina.

"You're holding me too tightly," she said.

"Aurelio shook my hand. He doesn't believe that I'm a murderer."

"Really now, David. It's much too hot to dance so closely."

"You're lovely," he said.

"David, please don't dance this way. People are watching us."

"Pretend that we're not dancing to this taco-calypso stuff—we're waltzing at a great ball in Czarist Russia."

"No one waltzes like *this*," she said. "David, darling, you're perspiring in my hair."

"Can you get away tonight?"

"I don't know."

"You can. Please, just for an hour—no one will miss us."

"I don't know, honestly. Maybe."

"I've phoned you, but you're never home."

"I'm home, but no one will let me speak to you."

"But you're here now. We'll meet later."

"David, the music has stopped."

"The music never stops when I'm holding you, Maria Cristina."

"You ass, stop dancing!"

"The holding never stops when I'm musicing you, Cristina Maria."

She laughed into his lapel. "David, please, there is no music now."

"Well, by God let the music commence."

"Daaa-vid!"

"Will you come with me later?"

"I'll try."

"Will you?"

"All right. Yes. I said yes, now will you let me go?"

"Baby, did you see me beat Felix today?"

"Please," she said.

"Take it easy, we've got music again, the band's playing. You saw me beat Felix."

"Well, yes."

"Did you see it or didn't you?"

"You played beautifully, but you didn't really beat him, you know. Maybe you'll play each other again sometime and—"

"I did beat him, Maria Cristina."

"He was hurt."

"Listen to me, I beat him."

"Why does it mean so much?"

"Later then?"

"Yes."

"Do you mean it?"

"Yes, David, yes, for God's sake, yes!"

"I changed my mind," he said.

ELEVEN

Felix Mondragon had put on a swimming suit and was doing some simple dives off of the low board. Swan, jackknife, backdive. He dived awkwardly but none of his admirers—Maria Cristina was among them— seemed to notice; they applauded and laughed at his jokes and reached out to lightly touch him. A hero. Felix was a real winner, David thought, the kind of man whom others regarded as triumphant immediately after they'd seen him defeated. He fogged minds with charm and style and confidence; he didn't have to actually win, he was beyond that, he was a personality. Now he did a pigeon-chested swan dive off the board.

David circled around the pool and stood on the edge of the crowd, not far from Maria Cristina. She did not notice him; she was watching Mondragon. Felix came up the ladder grinning, his hair in spiky bangs, his body wetly glistening and reflecting the colored lights. "*Que quebrar!*" he said senselessly, and everyone laughed.

"Nice dive, Felix," David said softly.

Mondragon grinned. "David, *amigo!*"

"You dive pretty well, *amigo*."

"I play," he said. "I have fun."

"Well, don't get hurt, *amigo*."

"David," Maria Cristina said quietly.

"How is your shoulder, *amigo*?" David asked.

Mondragon was still grinning. "Do you want me to get a note from my doctor?"

"Dive some more for us, Felix. We admire you."

"Why don't you get a swimming suit and join me?"

David shook his head. "No, not tonight. Some other time."

Mondragon shrugged.

"But don't go off the high board, *amigo*. You might get hurt."

"Oh, well, I shall probably try that soon. But why don't you show me how?"

"Well . . . " David said.

Maria Cristina moved close to him. "David, no, please, stop this."

"Maria Cristina doesn't want me to dive with you," David said.

"You son of a bitch!" she hissed.

"She's afraid I might get hurt."

Mondragon nodded. "I understand. American men are in the habit of obeying women."

David grinned. "I don't know. I suppose . . . Well, all right, Felix, I'll get a swimming suit."

David went into the bathhouse and sorted through the box of swimming suits until he found a pair of red trunks that fit. He changed and then sat on the bench to smoke a cigarette. A dramatic suspension; let Felix psyche up, gather his pride and sense of *machismo*. I'll test your charm and elegance, *amigo*.

He smoked his cigarette down to the filter and left the bathhouse. Most of the guests were gathered around the swimming pool now; they seemed to be in a nervously festive mood, like a sunny side bullfight crowd before the *Macareña* has been played, before the blood and the drunkenness. Reflections from the pool threw quivering spiders of light over their bright clothing and tinted their faces.

Mondragon, grinning again, met him near the scaffold and briefly embraced him. "*Suerte, amigo,*" he said. David tried to respond in a friendly way, but he had never been comfortable with the Latin custom of the *abrazo*, and he guessed that he had responded coldly and stiffly, in the usual gringo style. Score one for Mondragon.

"You go first."

"No, Felix, I'll follow you."

"Please, let me see what I must exceed."

David decided to skip all of the tension-building preliminaries on the low board and go directly into the blood-sport aspect of this competition. He would deny these assembled folk any artistic orchestration; the essence of the contest should not be disguised or dissembled.

He ascended the ladder. The platform seemed so much higher, and the pool so much smaller and farther away, at night. He could not clearly see the people below because of the glare of the Chinese lanterns, but he sensed their mass, and the weight of their interest.

He walked out to the end of the board. He had a touch of vertigo, but he tried to appear perfectly at ease. "Harry," he said.

"Yes?" The voice came from below and somewhere to his left.

"Can you dim the lights? They're too bright, I can't see very well."

"I can't dim them. I can turn them off."

"Do it."

David retreated to the platform. After a moment the lights were extinguished except for those beneath the pool's surface. He spent a minute pretending to limber up, but actually waiting for his eyes to adjust to the change in light. A few stars gradually emerged out of the blackness overhead. Below he saw the shimmering green glow of the water. And he could see the people gathered around the pool more clearly now, their pale, upturned faces, green-hued, and the pastels of their clothes. He saw Maria Cristina briefly, lost her, and could not find her again.

David went back out on the board and paced it off. They had received all the drama they were going to get from him.

"Are you waiting for someone to turn off the moon?" someone asked in Spanish.

He took two long steps, rose up and hit the end of the board. The recoil launched him upward and out over the water. He took two gulps of air and began his tuck, the glowing pool and the people and the stars revolving around him. He let his reflexes take over then except to remind himself that the board was very high and he was filled with adrenaline—it must be done leisurely. He completed one and one half revolutions, came out of the tuck, straightened and saw the glittering water rush up toward him, and then he hit. His entry was not good, he'd gone over too far, but it was a better dive than Mondragon could do if he practiced for a year. He plummeted down through the water too fast, breaking momentum with the curve of his body and then with his hands against the rough cement of the pool bottom. He felt twinges of pain in both wrists. The pool was simply not deep enough for that high board; he would have to enter with a flatter trajectory on future dives. He stayed down for a moment, looking up at the wobbling, mercury-like bubbles and the glare of the surface, and then he turned and kicked off the bottom. A few of the guests applauded as he swam to the ladder.

"Very nice, *amigo*," Mondragon called.

Felix climbed to the high platform. He flicked his fingers loosely and grinned—no one can grin as gaily as a scared Mexican, David thought—and then the board thumped and Mondragon was in the air.

It began as a fine swan dive and then rapidly fell to pieces. It began as a whole thing and then broke down into component parts—it was like watching a film with many of the frames missing. The splash rose five feet above the pool's surface. And the crowd began applauding before Mondragon reappeared. David was disgusted. What was the matter with these people? Couldn't they see? Couldn't they sense when a thing was done well?

David climbed the ladder and did a parody of Mondragon's dive. He began with a back-arched, toe-pointed, arm-spread swan and then made it fall apart, flailing his arms and legs, twisting his head aside, seemingly out of control, but then he swiftly turned it into a flip and entered the water feet first so cleanly that he knew that the splash was no bigger than if someone had dropped a twenty-pound rock into the pool.

Mondragon did an awful bowlegged jackknife and when he reached the ladder there were half a dozen persons waiting for him, and one handed him a drink. He threw it down in one gulp and grinned, and there was laughter and applause and a shrill *macho* yell.

What could you do?

David walked past the poolside crowd, looking at the faces. The Mexicans were restless, bright-eyed, agitated. There was no hostility in their glances, they were just very emotional. The Americans were colder. Charley Cole nodded. Mrs. Sanderson smiled tentatively. Harry Rudd winked. Maria Cristina was radiant, beautiful—she liked this, it excited her. Aurelio Santistevan was blinking rapidly. Evan Hughes met his eyes briefly and then glanced away. Vigil's mouth was stretched wide in his carnivore's grin.

David walked past all of them and went into the house and up the stairway and into a bedroom that,

judging by the scent, belonged to Norma Rudd. He
opened the French doors, moved out onto the small
balcony. There was a high wrought-iron railing that had
been twisted into flowers and swirling curlicues, and
through the grillework he could see the green glow of
the pool and the round, upturned faces of the crowd.
He mounted the railing. Here he was lower than on the
diving platform, and farther away from the water. The
dive would have to be very flat, almost horizontal, until
gravity pulled his upper body down for the entry. He felt
confident and a little crazy. He would have to pass over
at least twelve feet of the tiled pool apron before reach-
ing the water. It looked impossible. It wasn't, not if he
was aggressive.

He stood atop the railing, balancing, and then he
crouched and pushed off, driving through with his legs.
He was conscious of the tiles passing beneath him. His
head passed beyond the rim of the pool and he struck
the water in what was nearly a racing dive, flat and
hard. It took him a few seconds to realize that he had
not been hurt.

David sat on the edge of the pool, breathing deeply,
and then Mondragon appeared on the balcony. Felix
was all tawny skin and white teeth and bright-dark eyes,
and the people loved him, although they were beginning to fear for him, too. Felix was scared and everyone
sensed it.

You couldn't do this sort of thing if you were afraid;
fear made you tentative. You had to be aggressive, you
had to be a little *rabioso*, rabid.

Felix grinned gaily, climbed atop the railing, paused briefly to get his balance, and pushed off. At first it looked as though he might make it. His dive was flat enough, parallel to the pool apron. But he really hadn't driven through with his legs, hadn't kicked off violently enough. There had been something passive about the dive. He was stretched out flat when he hit the tiles. His head, thank God, was beyond the pool rim but his torso and legs hit with a dull, meaty sound and he skimmed off the tiles and into the pool. It appeared almost deliberate. It would have been comic except for the sound of the impact. He hit hard. Later, thinking about it, David decided that it was the wetness of the tiles that had saved Mondragon from serious injury. The smooth, wet-slick tiles had quickly converted most of the downward force into forward motion. Also, it helped that the impact was distributed over the length of his body. Mondragon had been stretched against the sky for an instant, resisting gravity, and he came forward and down, gaining momentum, and then hit the tiles with that awful sound and shot off into the water. His form held all the way; it was his most graceful dive of the night. "Ahhhh," the crowd said gutturally, some expelling air and some inhaling. There was that meaty sound and then the people, in almost perfect unison, sighing, "Ahhhh . . . "

"Ahhhh," David said with the others, and he dropped over the side, swam a few strokes and ducked beneath the surface. Mondragon, loose-limbed, hair flowing, was slowly drifting down toward the bottom of the pool. His eyes were open. The abrasions on his chest and legs emitted little puffs of blood that looked like dark brown smoke.

David lifted his head, inhaled, porpoised, dove downward. He cupped his right hand around Felix's jaw, turned, and pulled him to the surface and then over to the ladder. Doctor Pacheco and two other men were there and they lifted Mondragon out of the water and lay him chest up on the tiles.

And then David did a strange thing, an act that he was never quite able to understand. He turned and began swimming toward the shallow end of the pool. He swam hard and rhythmically, kicking, stroking, breathing in perfect synchronization—he had never swum so fast and well. He reached the wall at the shallow end, executed a good racing turn and started back. Nine or ten powerful strokes, another racing turn at the deep end, back again.

He swam fourteen laps before he lost the rhythm. He did not tire exactly. He still felt strong. But his coordination was a little off, he was a fraction early or a fraction late. He swam six more laps and then he went to the ladder and climbed out of the pool. Now he became aware of his fatigue. His chest heaved and there was a burning, metallic taste in his mouth and throat. His heart, unanchored it seemed, jumped around in his chest. Chlorine burned his eyes.

Mondragon was gone. And the party had lost cohesion; those guests who remained were gathered in small, almost furtive groups of three and four, and each group seemed to exclude all others.

David went into the bathhouse, changed into his clothing, and then went looking for Harry Rudd. He found him standing at the bar inside the house. There was just Harry and the servant Manuel.

"How is Mondragon?" David asked.

Harry slowly turned. "Jesus Christ," he said. "Why did you run?"

"I didn't run."

"Swim then, for Christ's sake. "Why did you *swim* away?"

"There was nothing for me to do."

"Shit, Dave, the kid was hurt."

"What did you do, Harry?"

"What?"

"Harry, what did you do to help Mondragon? After I pulled him over to the ladder."

"I was there, goddamn it."

"But what did you do?"

"I didn't do anything, but I was available to help."

"Sure," David said. "Did Dr. Pacheco consult with you or was he able to attend to the patient all by himself?"

"Screw this, I'm not in the mood for it."

"Neither am I. Still, you should have come swimming with me, Harry, instead of standing around and gawking at the remains."

"Listen, what's the matter with you tonight?"

"I wonder."

"Listen, you pushed Felix off that balcony railing the same as if you'd shoved him with your hands."

"What?"

"That's right. Don't attempt to deny it. I don't mind telling you that I was shocked—I didn't believe that you were capable of that kind of brutality."

David laughed. "Shocked, huh? That's beautiful, Harry. Well, what the hell did you expect of someone who throws women off cliffs?"

"I didn't mean that."

"Yes, you did."

David turned and walked toward the doorway. He glanced over at the buffet table. He was very hungry but he could not eat here and now; it would be too "brutal." He was expected to feel guilty and guilt was known to kill the appetite. He wondered how many people still at the party were hungry but could not eat because there had been an accident. You simply did not stuff food in your mouth soon after someone had been hurt.

He went outside and moved from group to group, asking if anyone knew where Maria Cristina had gone. People were not exactly impolite, but there was a flat, dull look in their eyes and their voices were without inflection. It was as if David's membership in a club with very low standards had been revoked. He was not hurt or angry; he just felt a little less real than he had this morning.

Well, he thought, if there was ever a night to get drooling, fall-down drunk, this is it.

TWELVE

David dreamed that he was drinking cold water from a veined marble fountain in a park. He could hear wind in the leaves overhead. Shade-spattered sunlight moved back and forth over the grass. Children shouted, happy and angry. He drank. He could see sparkling motes in the mushroom of water, stars, planets, moons, comets, a whole galaxy. He swallowed a galaxy and a new one appeared. The water was so cold that it hurt his throat and eyes. He drank until his breath was gone, rested for a moment and then drank again, but he could not quench his thirst.

The shadows lengthened, the children went away, night came. It was very cold in the park and snow was falling. The trees were bare now and snow-powdered dead leaves rustled over the dried grass. The mushroom of water froze.

David awakened slowly. It was early in the morning; there were shadows, cocks crowed, church bells rang for early Mass. Señora Gonzales was noisily scrubbing down the sidewalk and cobblestones in front of the building. A vendor at the far end of the street was chanting, "*Leche, crema, están frías, leche, crema, fría y dulce.*" The wooden wheels of the vendor's cart clattered on the cobblestones. David could think of nothing he wanted and needed more than a quart of milk, cold and sweet, but he knew that the old man dipped the milk out of steel ten-gallon cans—it was not pasteurized.

He was sick. He had the worst hangover of his life. His hands trembled, he was nauseated, his head ached. He drank two glasses of water, a glass of orange juice, and a cup of coffee, and then promptly vomited.

Dear body: I am so very sorry.

The sea. He pulled on cut-off Levi's, stepped into sandals, and went down the stairs. The sidewalk and cobblestones in front of the building were wet. A neighbor child, with milk on her upper lip, watched him from across the street.

"*Buenos días,* Flor," David said.

"*Buenos días, señor,*" she solemnly replied.

He walked through the quiet streets of the village and down the path toward the sea.

He was sick and it was like walking in a nightmare; everything, the town and sky, grass, trees, the ocean, vibrated with a subtle menace. Several times he thought he saw motion out of the corner of his eye, but when he turned there was nothing there.

He passed from shadow into sunlight. Seagulls flew toward him, mewing for bread. He showed them that his hands were empty.

He reached the beach and walked north through the deep, still-cool sand. The stubborn gulls glided after him, tilting their wings, riding the breeze like cleverly made paper airplanes.

David kicked off his sandals, dropped his wallet on the sand, and waded out into the sea. The water was warm, mucoid, clinging; it seemed to have a different texture today. He did not like its touch. The water seemed slimy. That was ridiculous. But it did look slimy, and it felt slimy, like a gently heaving semi-jelly. His mind invested the sea with mysterious horrors. Something brushed his leg and he leaped aside, involuntarily groaning. He saw that it was only a yellowish mass of seaweed. He paused, shivering. He had been certain that the weed was part of a human body, a deliquescent arm or leg. No, he could not swim in this putrid slime today. He was sick, he was anxious, and he wanted to do something that was wholly clean and did not have any obscure alliances with death.

The little girl, Flor, was still sitting on the curbstone. "*Señor,*" she said quietly.

He paused and looked down at her. She was very young, no more than nine or ten, but he could see an eighty-year-old witch waiting behind her eyes. He was half tempted to lean down and brush the flaky milk crust off her upper lip.

"The police," she said.

"Where?"

"In your house."

"Why are they there?"

"I don't know."

"Well," he said. He glanced up toward his balcony and then down the street. A police car was parked near the corner.

"I don't like them," the girl said.

"I don't like them either, Flor."

"Run away."

"No, I don't think so."

David crossed the street, walking slowly up the stairway, paused for a moment on the landing—perhaps he should run—and then pushed open the door to his room.

"Hello, Vigil," he said.

"Captain."

"Sorry. Captain Vigil."

Vigil was sitting on the wooden crate that David used for a desk. He was smiling. A uniformed policeman, his hand resting casually—or perhaps not so casually—on the butt of his holstered revolver, was standing near the French doors.

"Is this it?" David asked.

"I think it is," Vigil said gently. "Close the door."

David shut the door, crossed the room, and sat on the floor with his back against the wall. He closed his eyes.

"You look awful," Vigil said. "You look like you had a very bad night."

"You don't know the half of it," David said.

"I know all of it."

"I suppose you do. I assumed that I've been watched."

"I'm curious—why didn't you run?"

"Just now, you mean?"

"During the last few weeks."

"I thought about it. But there was no place to run to."

"The States."

"You know what's waiting for me there."

"Nothing is waiting for you there."

David considered opening his eyes, but he was just too sick and tired and indifferent. "The indictments," he said.

"The State of Florida dropped the charge. There was a pretrial hearing for your friend in the adventure, and the judge ruled that certain evidence could not be introduced because of an illegal search and seizure."

"Christ," David said wearily. "Now you tell me. What about the federal indictment?"

"It's still on the books, valid I believe, but without the Florida charge . . . Flight to avoid prosecution can't be very serious if there is no prosecution. There is nothing to worry about there."

"But there is something to worry about here."

"That is correct."

"Why didn't you tell me the truth about this?" David asked. Then: "Never mind, I know."

"I didn't want you to leave Mexico."

"Right."

"I didn't have enough evidence to arrest you."

"But you do now?"

"Yes."

"Am I under arrest then?"

"Yes."

"I didn't kill her, Vigil. I swear I didn't."

"David, I like you. Do you believe me?"

"No."

"But it's true, I do like you." His voice was soft and lilting, as if he were talking to a child. "You are basically an honest man, I believe, and a good one. And you have courage. I like that."

"I didn't do it," David said tiredly. "And I'm not going to tell you that I did."

"The game is over. You played it well, but now you must tell me the truth. Relieve the terrible pressure, free yourself of your guilt and remorse and fear. Give me a share of your burden, David, your pain. Tell me, I'll understand—perhaps only a policeman can understand. Now, now is the time to open your heart."

David smiled faintly. "I would, Vigil, really I would open my heart—but I didn't do it."

"I can understand how it happened," Vigil said. "I can imagine the chain of circumstances, visualize the nightmare sequence of action you found yourself committed to. I do understand. More than that, I sympathize. It could happen to anyone."

"I didn't do it."

"David, open your eyes."

"I don't want to. I like it here in the dark."

"Open your eyes and look at me."

"I've seen enough, I'm blind. And deaf. If you really do like me, Vigil, you'll assure that I'm taken care of for the rest of my life. Get me a job selling lottery tickets."

"David, I insist that you look at me."

Reluctantly, he opened his eyes. Vigil was wearing a pale blue veil, the girl's veil.

"Very pretty, but you ought to pluck your eyebrows."

"We found it here in this room, concealed beneath a loose tile."

"You found it in your hip pocket," David said.

"We missed it on our earlier search."

"That's because it wasn't here then."

"Why did you keep this veil? Was it some kind of ghastly memento? Was it an unconscious wish to be apprehended and punished?" He removed the veil.

"Captain Vigil, beat me up, take me to jail, whatever you should do, but don't ask me to swallow any more horseshit. Okay?"

Vigil rose to his feet and approached. "All right," he said. "We'll be going now."

David stood up. "Can I get dressed and take a few things with me?"

"Yes."

When David stood up, Vigil swiftly stepped forward and hit him on the mouth, not too hard, not viciously, just firmly enough to snap his head back and cut his lip; hard enough to instruct him that he could no longer consider himself the equal of policemen, of free men, and that along with his freedom they intended to confiscate his pride and manhood.

The uniformed policeman had warily moved off to the side, his hand still resting on the butt of his revolver.

Vigil said, "A friend informed me last night that this veil was concealed in your room."

"Your friend or my friend?"

"He tripped on a tile and exposed the veil."

"Are you serious?"

"Haven't you yet learned that I am a serious man?"

"Who is this . . . informer?"

"He has asked that his identity be concealed."

"Of course. Jesus. Listen, I bring people up here. And anyone could enter while I'm out, the door doesn't lock. Someone has framed me, Vigil, and if it isn't you, it's this 'friend.'"

Vigil smiled. "Do you think this is a movie?"

"Good God, man, listen—the one who told you he found the veil here is the killer. He planted it here. Can't you see that?"

"Get dressed."

"Who was it? Tell me. I have a right to face my accuser."

Vigil slapped him twice. "Get dressed."

THIRTEEN

The combination police station, jail, and Mexican Army barracks were located on a narrow cobbled street near the center of the old section of town. It had been a fort during the days when pirates still threatened this coast, and it had not been modernized much since then; there were no glass windows, just gun slits of various dimensions and, as he learned, the prisoners' wing contained primitive electrical and plumbing systems. The fort occupied an entire city block. It was square with an open space in the middle the size of a pair of tennis courts. The army occupied the interior of two of the walls for their offices and barracks; the west and north walls comprised the police station and jail.

David had walked past the old fort two or three times a week to the post office to inquire about letters which rarely arrived. After a time he had ceased to consciously observe it; it became as familiarly dull as everything else along the route, his own street, the corner *bodegas,* the sidewalk carts selling sausages and tripe and ices and fruit-flavored drinks, the narrow,

hole-in-the-wall cantina in which the bar ran the length
of one wall and a urinal trough extended the length
of the wall opposite, the stony, empty lot where kids
played soccer, and the Grecian-Toltec post office itself,
with its huge fresco which sentimentally, in comic-book
style, pictured the history of Mexico from Quetzalcoatl
through the American Marine assault on Chapultepec
castle. (The military cadets, the "boy heroes," were
pictured wrapped in flags as they leaped from a parapet—the Mexican concept of triumph; elegant suicide.)
For a long time David disliked that fresco, then he felt
affection for it, and finally he did not see it anymore,
in the same way as he'd ceased being aware of the
old fort.

But he saw the fort clearly enough today. Vigil and
the uniformed policeman walked him along the west
wall. He could smell the sun-heated stones. He noticed
the lichens that grew in the crevices. He saw wasps
crawling in and out of holes in the chalky mortar.

The policemen led him up four stone steps and
through thick double doors into the police station. It
was an enormous rectangular room with stone floor
and walls and a very high stone ceiling. It was cold and
damp and musty-smelling, like a pre-Columbian tomb
he had once visited.

There were a dozen desks scattered around the
room, green filing cabinets, an iron-barred cabinet which
contained pistols and rifles and compact automatic
weapons, electric fans, loose paper, dirt, flies, more
wasps, and a cold institutional languor. A fat policeman

typed with two fingers. A woman clerk held a bottle of cola in one hand and a half-eaten taco in the other. Clusters of miserable civilians, mostly women and children, sat on benches against the wall; they looked as though they had been waiting a long time and expected to wait longer still. At first David had the feeling that this place was like a tomb, but now it seemed that he was inside a kind of secular church. The dim light, the ancient stone walls, echoes, penitents and priests, the prevailing emotions—fear, guilt, anguish, remorse, the desperate hope of pity and absolution.

He was guided to a far corner of the room and halted before a desk. On the desk there was a sign:

Luis de Borbolla
JEFE DE GUARDAS

The man standing behind the desk was about fifty years old, heavy, jowly, thick-lipped, with salt and pepper hair and moustache. His khaki uniform was soiled. He had not shaved in three or four days. His left hand and arm were dead, shrunken; it looked as if the mummified arm of a child had somehow been grafted onto his adult torso. In his other hand he held what appeared to be a slender, yard-long blackjack. The stick was made of tightly woven leather and gradually thickened until it was about two inches in diameter at the end. David was certain that the last few inches were filled with lead shot. He looked at the face of Luis de Borbolla, at his withered arm, at the blackjack, and he felt a surge of dread that seemed to dissolve the bones in his legs. His knees buckled slightly.

Another jail guard stood nearby, a young, moon-faced Indian with straight, bowl-cut, blue-black hair and muddy Indian eyes. The Indian smiled at him. Half of his front teeth were gone.

"No papers on this one," Vigil said in Spanish. "Not yet."

Luis de Borbolla, Chief of Guards, slowly and contemptuously looked at David.

"Vigil, what do you mean no papers?" David asked.

"It means that you are not being officially registered at this hotel."

"And what does *that* mean?"

"Watch your tongue here. Do as you're commanded. When you're ready to talk to me, inform one of the guards."

"You're *leaving?*"

Vigil looked at him curiously, mockingly. "David, this is jail. Don't ask me to hold your hand."

Vigil and the uniformed policeman left.

"Empty your pockets," Luis de Borbolla demanded. He had a surprising voice, a clear, boyish tenor.

Borbolla, with his good hand, removed the money from David's wallet, counted the money into two piles like a man dealing cards, gave the small sheaf of bills to the Indian, and then folded the other sheaf and put it in his pocket.

David turned and glanced around the room to see if anyone had observed the theft. The female clerk, watching him, finished her taco and then drank from the cola bottle.

"Okay, gringo sheet," Borbolla said, gesturing toward a heavy wooden door with his stick.

The Indian went through the door first, then David, and then Borbolla who shut and locked the door behind him. "Okay, you focker," Borbolla said.

It was a long, bare stone room. There was the door they had entered through, a door in the wall to the left which David assumed opened onto the street, and another door to the right which probably led into the courtyard.

The Indian was smiling.

David hesitantly returned the smile. He felt that he could trust the Indian.

"One dirty focker this," Barbolla said.

The Indian grinned.

David saw motion out of the corner of his eye and he began to turn. Borbolla rolled his wrist easily, like flipping an egg, and his leather stick flexed, curved into a bow, paused for an instant at the end of backlash, then whipped forward, gathering speed.

David watched, not understanding. The heavy end of the blackjack struck him on the muscle at the forward point of his left shoulder. There was a tingling electric pain and then a hot-needled numbness and then his arm was dead.

The pleasant-faced Indian was smiling and nodding at him.

Borbolla rolled his wrist again, and again the stick bowed, froze for a microsecond, and then whipped forward. David's pain and bewilderment slowed his reflexes. The heavy end of the blackjack struck his other shoulder, paralyzing the nerve. He tried to lift his arms, to fight, but he could not. Both of his arms were deadened. He heard himself cursing. Then the Indian's round, smiling face filled his field of vision. Maybe the Indian would help him. The muscles tensed in the Indian's jaw, his smile became a grimace, his eyes were abstracted.

David was lying on the cool stone floor. A few crucial seconds were missing from his life. He sat up. He did not understand. Now he saw the Indian's face again, above him. The man was not smiling now; he was very serious, very intent, and his tongue made a bulge in his cheek. Then, almost magically, a fist appeared and rapidly grew large. The back of David's head struck the stone floor. Again he lost the few precious seconds that night have provided continuity, sense, to what was happening to him. He was choking on blood. Blood filled his throat, his sinuses, gushed from his nose. He was drowning. He choked, he could not breathe. His body, beyond control of his mind now, spasmed and he was sitting erect. He coughed violently and his vision was filled with red mist, a sparkling cloud that absurdly reminded him of cotton candy.

He felt himself being lifted; he was weightless, floating. A tall rectangle of blinding light. Fresh air. Then he was running through the block of light—no, he had been propelled—and he was stumbling, top-heavy, through a sun-drenched desert. He ran, losing balance, recovering.

Nothing grew on this desert; it was all ashy dust, chalky pebbles, furnace winds. The field of gray ash rushed up toward him. He was unable to break the fall with his hands. He had no hands, no arms.

He tasted the ashy soil, his blood. Twisted his head aside so that he could breathe. What the hell? Jesus. What was going on? Borbolla, you focker . . . They weren't human. Animals.

David, without attempting to use his arms, struggled erect. He looked around. The prison courtyard was surrounded by the high stone walls. There was a guard in the southeast turret.

It was close to noon now; the sun was overhead, and thirty or forty prisoners were gathered in a dark triangle of shade in the corner. They all wore civilian clothes. There was just enough shade to contain all of them; any newcomer would have to sit partly in sunlight. They sat together in the gray dust, smoking silently, watching him. No one made a gesture of pity or welcome.

His nose was streaming blood. Blood fell in heavy drops and clotted like coins in the dust. He pinched his nostrils between thumb and forefinger. He felt drunk, remote from his surroundings and from himself. There was not much pain yet, just numbness here and there which guaranteed pain when his adrenal rage and fear wore off.

The entire courtyard was glazed sunlight and ashy dust except for the wedge of shadow where his fellow prisoners sat, and a single, startling tree in the precise center of the arena. No one sat in the tree's shade.

Blood was crawling down his forearm in thin, crooked rivulets. "Oh, goddamn," he said softly. He had a drunken, nostalgic craving for lucidity. The sun made him sick and dizzy. Blood everywhere, on his face, hands, clothing, blood thickening into moist dark clots in the dust.

David walked slowly toward the tree. He could not walk in a straight line. The prisoners watched silently. Go to hell, this isn't any kind of theater, I'm hurt.

He crawled beneath the lower branches of the tree, leaned back against the trunk, and tested his right arm. It moved, it worked, not well but it worked. He scooped up a handful of dust and carefully stuffed it into his nostrils. Vigil, you are not a civilized man. You knew what was going to happen, you wanted it to happen, and you walked away.

David tilted his head back and remained motionless for five or ten minutes and then he heard footsteps, a voice, and he cocked his head and opened his eyes.

"How're you doing?" A young American, under twenty-five, with crickets in his voice. "I'm Max."

"Hi, Max," David said. "Buzz off, Max."

"You're looking at my bare feet. They stole my shoes. Three-hundred-dollar shoes, you can't expect that they'll let you keep them. They took my Rolex Oyster, too, and some gold rings I had."

"Jesus," David said.

"Starting to hurt?"

"Like hell."

"Did they kick you?"

"I don't think so. No."

"A few weeks ago they ruptured the spleen of a drunk."

"Oh, well, a drunk . . . "

"That Huerta's got a hell of a right hand, don't he?"

"Who's Huerta?"

"The young one."

"The Indian?"

"Yeah."

"He looks so innocent."

"He looks like a fat girl who doesn't want you to hurt her feelings."

"My arms won't function properly," David said.

"Luis's work. He's a genius. He can kill a fly with that super blackjack of his without touching the wall. Some advice for you—if he ever goes to use that thing on you again, stand still. Freeze. He'll hurt you, but he won't break anything. If you move, you'll mess up his aim and maybe get a crushed shoulder joint or broken hip."

"This is insane."

"Sure."

"I mean, Jesus—unmotivated."

"That was just the softening-up. A premature warning. They won't bother you again unless you get out of line."

"Are my arms ruined?"

"Not if Luis hit you the way he wanted to. Your arms will come around. But that's Luis's favorite trick. He likes to see useless arms on other people."

"I can't believe this."

"What did they get you for? That's a rude question but we're Americans."

"Murder," David said.

Max raised his eyebrows. "Trouble, guy. I'm here for dope."

"I'm innocent."

"I'm not. I was betrayed by the Mexican Army, the whole goddamn Mexican Army. We paid off, paid very good, and here I am. But I'll be out soon. I work for a big outfit. We got millions. I make sixty, seventy thousand a year. Look at this shirt—silk. This jacket? Real Harris tweed. The pants cost me a C. It's all filthy now, but you can see the quality. They took my watch and my shoes."

"I was in dope once," David said.

"Yeah? Where?"

"Florida. The Keys."

"That's the spot. Our operation's going to move there. You can't trust the Mexican cops or army anymore. Anyway, no one wants to smoke the Mexican shit anymore, it's deadly with herbicides, everyone wants Columbian grass."

"I got caught," David said. "First time."

Max nodded. "You got to have an organization behind you."

"They didn't book me just now," David said. "They didn't do any paperwork. What does that mean?"

"They didn't book me properly either. That's because we're a rich outfit and they don't want records on me for when we pay off. It's just business. They don't rough me up. I'm valuable property. Are you rich?"

"No."

"You got rich, powerful friends?"

"I guess not."

"Okay, I'll be your rich and powerful friend, then."

"Sure."

"Come on with me. We'll go sit in the shade of the wall."

"I'm already in the shade."

"You can't stay here. There's a rule that no prisoners can come around this tree."

"Why?"

"It's a rule. If Luis or the Indian kid catches you here you'll get knocked around again."

"That doesn't make sense."

"Look, you've got to start thinking logically. If they catch you under that tree they'll pound you around the head. So you move."

"That isn't logical!"

"It's logical to move, very logical."

Max led him across the yard to a wedge of shade. The shadow gradually diminished and a new shadow appeared at the base of the opposite wall. The prisoners, except for David and Max, crossed the courtyard.

"Is that all you do, chase shadows all day?" David asked.

"Just about. How're you feeling?"

"What's the routine in this dungeon?"

"Tortillas and beans at six in the morning. Then we come out into the yard and stay until six at night. There isn't any work. For dinner we get tortillas and beans

again, and sometimes a bowl of soup or stew. It stinks.
I mean, you can't smell and eat at the same time. I don't
eat the stuff. I give one of the guards some money and he
brings me in some real food. Have you got any money?"

"No. They took all of it."

"Have your friends bring you some money when
they visit. You can't hardly get by in here without a
little money. A little money, a little power. A lot of
money, a lot of power. Okay? We sleep four or five to a
tiny stone room. There are bugs in the mattresses and
blankets. The plumbing backs up and so sometimes
you sleep in shit."

"I don't think I can take it," David said.

"You'll take it."

"I'll escape."

"I wouldn't try it."

"Well, you're rich," David said sarcastically.

"It could be done. The security here's a joke. But if
they catch you trying it, you die. They don't take prisoners prisoner here."

"I think my nose is broken."

"It looks like it. Look, I'll be getting out in a couple
of days. Anyone you want me to get in touch with?"

David gave him the names of Dr. Pacheco, Harry
Rudd, Maria Cristina, and Chucho. "Tell them to come
and see me."

"Sure. Write down the names for me later. Something else; I won't have much money left when they get
through bleeding me. But I can give you a little. Who
should I pass it to?"

"Chucho, the kid," David said, knowing that there would not be any money.

"Right. I can maybe spare a couple hundred. That'll take care of smokes and eats. I got plenty of money back in the States. I got a house in San Diego, and a boat—a Bertram. When I go to Vegas to gamble it's all comp. I don't pay for nothing. Room, meals, drinks, hookers, it's all comp."

"Shut up," David said.

"You don't believe me. I got a Caddy and a Lincoln, and I'm restoring an old Packard. I got twenty-five cashmere sweaters."

"Shut up. I want to sleep."

"You shouldn't fall asleep in the sun," Max said. "Come on, we'll cross over."

FOURTEEN

Late Wednesday afternoon David was sitting beneath the courtyard tree when he saw Huerta walking toward him. Puffs of dust detonated at his boot heels. David had made a point of sitting beneath the tree because the pain of a beating could hardly exceed the mental pain of knowing that he'd permitted demented automatons to select even the places where he might rest. Now he expected a kick in the face, but Huerta simply told him to get up, there was a visitor.

A door on the north wall of the courtyard led into a room which the prisoners called "the bird cage." There was no furniture in the dirty ten-by-twelve room, no windows, just three rough stone walls, the door, and in front, running from wall to wall, a tight-meshed wire screen. You looked through the screen into a long corridor. A sleepy guard sat in the corner.

David waited nervously for five minutes and then he heard the door at the far end of the corridor open and close. He dropped his cigarette because he did not want his visitor, whoever it was, to see that his hands were trembling.

123

Doctor Pacheco's golf shoes clicked on the stone floor. Walking slowly toward David, he shook his head and laughed, said, "A veritable dungeon." He stopped in front of the screen and looked at David. "Home is where the corpus is." He wore a tan short-sleeved sport shirt, chocolate brown slacks, brown and white golf shoes, and a cream-colored beret. There was a golf glove on his right hand. The clothes were new and expensive, but they did not fit properly, emphasizing his dwarfish physique.

"Hello, Paco," David said.

"Well, look," Pacheco said, still grinning. "See what has happened to our blue-eyed boy."

"Thanks for coming to see me."

"It's nothing. I'm between a gall bladder and golf."

"I didn't know you were a golfer."

"I'm learning. Did they beat you severely around the head?"

"Yes."

"Shocking," Pacheco said with his barracuda grin.

"It really isn't funny."

"I know, I know, it's tragic. God, what remains after the world has brutalized Tom Sawyer! Have we actually come to that? Who would dare harm a blue-eyed, fair-haired, barefoot boy from the solid Midwest? Pike in the lake and pheasants in the corn. A Christmas goose. Fireflies in bottles. Angleworms dropped down the blouses of giggly girls. Freckles everywhere."

"Paco . . ."

"Why did you want to see me?"

"Why! Because I need help."

"That does appear to be so."

"I've got to get out of here."

"And how do you propose to do that?"

"I don't know. Maybe someone could post bond."

"Someone? Who is this someone? Not me certainly."

"Okay."

"Have you appeared before a magistrate?"

"No."

"Then forget the thought of bail for now."

"Paco, you have influence, maybe you could talk to people. Find out what's going on, what's going to happen to me."

"Do you play golf?" Pacheco asked.

David saw how it was going to be. He relaxed and smiled. "I've played a little."

"I have a horrendous slice, I hit boomerang drives."

"That's because you're so short. You stand too close to the ball."

"Imagine that."

"That and your clothes. It's impossible to hit the ball straight when you're wearing a pimp outfit."

"Yes, yes, well, I must go. It wouldn't do to stand here talking to a depraved convict while rich, important people wait at the first tee."

"So long, Paco."

"Don't you think you should address me as Dr. Pacheco? Felons usually do."

"Sorry."

Pacheco turned and started down the corridor.

"Doctor Pacheco," David called.

He stopped, looked back.

"You've got the golf glove on the wrong hand."

"What?"

"You're right-handed. The glove should go on your left hand."

"Oh. Thank you."

"Not at all, Dr. Pacheco."

Later in the day he was returned to the bird cage. Maria Cristina was waiting on the other side of the screen. She wore a short, sleeveless white dress, high-heeled shoes, a red coral necklace, and a matching coral and silver bracelet. She smelled of the sun.

"Thank you for coming," David said.

"That Max character telephoned me. What are you *doing* in this place, David?"

"I think I've been arrested for murder."

"Oh, what nonsense! They'll get it all straightened out soon, you'll see. What happened to your face?"

"The guards beat me up."

She laughed. "Oh, David, stop playing James Cagney."

"I slipped in the shower."

"Careless boy."

"Did you know where I was? Before Max phoned you?"

"No, no one seemed to know anything. You just vanished."

"There was nothing in the newspapers?"

She shook her head.

"Maybe I haven't been officially arrested for murder."

"Of course not."

"This might be a kind of preventative detention."

"Well, whatever, it's absurd."

"How is Felix?"

"He's out of the hospital. He has some broken ribs and some simply awful bruises, but he's all right."

"When are you returning to school?"

"I'm leaving tomorrow morning. I can't stay with you much longer. I have to pack."

"Will you talk to your father for me? He has a lot of power in this town."

"Well, of course, I'll talk to him. But I don't know. He doesn't like you very much, David."

"Talk to him anyway, okay?"

"Yes. And I must go now, really. Please don't be gloomy. You'll be out of this horrid place soon, darling, and it will all seem like a hilarious joke then."

"An adventure."

"Exactly."

"It's already starting to seem funny."

"That's the spirit. Pessimism has never solved anything."

"Well, thank you for coming, Maria Cristina."

"I would have come sooner if I had known. Bye-bye, write to me, won't you?"

"Sure."

She smiled, kissed her fingertips, waved them at David, and then turned and walked down the corridor.

The next morning David had another visitor.

"What happened to your face?" Harry Rudd asked.

"One of the guards beat me up."

"What for?"

"No special reason."

"He must have had a reason."

"No reason, Harry."

"What about those welts on your arms?"

"These? I don't know—insects, spiders, centipedes."

"Aw, Jesus Christ, Davey."

"This ain't the Hilton."

"Just look at what you got yourself into."

"I didn't get myself into this."

"A stinking cesspool."

"I don't know what's going on, what Vigil's up to. Maybe he intends to let me soften up here for a couple of weeks and then go for a confession. I don't know. But I'm not booked into this hotel, Harry, and I haven't been brought before a judge, and I haven't been charged with any crime, there's no paper on me, technically I'm not even here. And yet I can have visitors."

"You know the Mexicans, kid. They improvise a lot."

"How did you learn I was here?"

"That creep came to the house last night."

"Max?"

"Yeah."

"It just doesn't make sense."

"It makes sense all right. I talked to Vigil this morning. He told me about the veil."

"Sure, the veil. That son of a bitch planted the veil in my room."

"Hey, Dave, cut the crap now, huh?"

"What?"

"Look, I believed you, nearly everyone believed you. But we just aren't going to accept any more of your lies."

"Harry . . . "

"You killed the girl, you got caught, and so why don't you stand up like a man and take the heat? Got that? Stop whining about how you're innocent and how the guards slap you around and your insect bites."

"Good-bye, Harry."

"Vigil told me about your record in the States. A dope smuggler, and now a killer. Once a punk always a punk."

"Get out of here," David said.

"You sure suckered me, pal. I bought your whole routine. I brought you into my house, I trusted you, I treated you like a son. You were like my own blood to me. But you're nothing but a cheap punk, a lying hustler, and . . . "

And then David was amazed to see Harry begin to weep. His face contorted and grew red, and he pawed clumsily at his eyes, and though he tried to speak his words were so slurred by emotion that David could not understand. Harry cried helplessly for a moment and then turned and walked down the corridor.

Chucho visited him three days later. He was wearing a new pair of shiny black patent-leather shoes with three-inch heels. The shoes made him look taller, of course, and thinner, and they exaggerated the *macho* swagger of his walk. He stopped on the other side of the mesh screen, folded his arms, and grinned.

"Where have you been, you little bastard?"

"Hey, I feel better with you behind that screen like a wild animal, man," Chucho said. "You are one crazy gringo gangster. Al Capone. John Dillinger. You a dangerous hoodlum, man."

"Nice shoes," David said.

"You like them? Twelve-hundred pesos."

"I'm dying in here, I can't buy food, I can't buy cigarettes, and you spend sixty dollars on a pair of shoes."

Chucho stepped back on mock fear. "*Un criminal! Un bruto! Un animal!* Babyface Nelson, man."

"Have you got any money left?"

"Sure, we're rich, man. I give you a little cigarette money before I go."

"Thanks a lot."

Chucho hooked a thumb toward the guard. "He know English?"

"No."

"Okay. Okay, Flaco. I'm gonna get you out of this here nasty place."

"Sure."

"You are gonna escape, man. I'm gonna bust you outta here like hoodlums in the movies."

"You stupid shit."

"Hey, you think I'm kidding? I got the money for bribes. I just got to work out the details, you know, and *negociar* with the right guys."

"Where did you get the money?"

"That Max, he gave me five hundred dollars."

"Christ. I thought he was all mouth."

"I raised eighteen hundred dollars myself."

"How?"

"I robbed the Nicholson place myself."

"You should be in here and I should be outside."

"A crazy wild beast in the cage."

"How much money is left?"

"You want to hear in pesos or dollars?"

"I don't care, just tell me."

Chucho shook a cigarette loose from the package, stuck it in the corner of his mouth, lit a match and exhaled a cloud of smoke toward the ceiling. "A two, man, A two. A one. A zero."

"Twenty-two hundred and ten dollars? And that's enough to get me out of here?"

"Not out the front door. But I'm gonna get you outta this zoo, baby. Over the wall."

"You're crazy."

"Stay cool. I could have got you out without this money, but this way they don't shoot you as many times." He grinned.

FIFTEEN

The square, high-ceilinged kitchen was hot and humid; steam fogged the air and condensed into clear drops of water on the stone walls. There was a stink of greasy food, and garbage, and excrement—the jail plumbing was very old, usually clogged, and toilet wastes constantly backed up through the kitchen drains, boiled up out of the sinks and floor grille. David was nauseated by the stench. He had been nauseated every morning, noon, and evening for three days, ever since being assigned (as Chucho had arranged) to the kitchen slop and scrub detail.

Now, kneeling on the floor, he sprayed a jet of steam onto a soot-blackened iron kettle. The steam mushroomed; he felt a blast of heat. He gave it another burst, lowered the steam gun, and scrubbed the inside of the kettle with a ball of steel wool.

He felt a light touch on his shoulder and turned. Perez, as hard and thin as a ferret.

"Okay?" Perez asked.

David glanced at his watch. "Twenty more minutes."

Perez nodded and drifted away.

David had been made captain of the kitchen clean-up crew and had kept the men an hour or ninety minutes late for the past three nights. He needed darkness for his escape. The others, Perez, Trujillo, and Rios, did not mind; they could steal a little extra food; and in this place, where idleness was hell, work seemed an acceptable purgatory.

He worked for a few more minutes, stood, wiped his hands on a dirty towel, and casually walked through the kitchen door and out into the dimly lit hallway. The comparatively cooler air here was chilling.

The guard's chair was empty, as Chucho had promised. ("'Mano, you got to move—he ain't gone long.")

David turned right and walked swiftly down the hallway. Ancient rock-dust smell, time, and defeat encapsulated in these thick stone walls—an angular tomb.

He hesitated briefly in front of the door leading out into the courtyard ("It's gonna be open, man, but not for long"), turned the tarnished brass knob, and pushed. The heavy door swung open easily, silently, as if mounted on an intricate system of ball bearings instead of old iron hinges.

He stepped outside and quickly closed the door behind him. In a shadow but feeling exposed—this was death country at night.

The courtyard: a slanting, light rain coming past the floodlights; the lone tree a shadow multiplying itself half a dozen times in other, paler shadows; stone walls tilting inward with perspective; the cylindrical guard tower looking like a lighthouse.

Oh, Jesus, no, impossible.

It was not too late to quit, he could return to the kitchen in time. This was suicide. Treachery—he would be betrayed, by Chucho, by the hall guard and the tower guard, by fate. You could not buy justice. His luck had been so bad for so long . . .

He pressed his back against the wall, willing the shadows to embrace him. I can't do it, I just can't do it.

The muddy courtyard looked like a little square of desert enclosed by steep stone cliffs. An illuminated graveyard.

An automobile horn sounded beyond the wall. Life continued out there.

Now he heard the bolt being thrown in the door. It was too late to return to the safety of the jail and— he glanced at his watch—almost too late to go forward with the escape. Where was Chucho? ("'Mano, it costs lots of money for just a couple minutes, man. You go overtime and them people are gonna shoot you.")

He saw something out of the corner of his eye, turned fearfully, and saw the rope snaking down through the air a few yards to his left, writhing like something alive, and then it slapped hard against the wall.

He wiped his hands on his trousers, knowing that he did not possess the strength to climb it now. Yesterday or tomorrow, yes, but now he felt so faint and sweaty-sick that it seemed an impossible task. He weakly gripped the rope: it was thick, that was good, and was made with a rough hemp. He tried climbing, without hope, and was surprised to find it easy; he had more than enough strength, there was no strain at all, and he was hardly aware of floating up fifteen feet and surmounting the low parapet. He was drunk on adrenaline.

Halfway across the flat roof he stopped and looked toward the dimly lit guard tower. The guard, a fat-faced man, was staring at him. Their eyes met across forty yards of space. David heard Chucho's voice from below on the street—"Man, where are you? Come on!" The guard swiveled the heavy, black .50 caliber machine gun and sighted down the barrel. He held that position for a moment, then tilted his head back, closed his eyes, and silently laughed.

David moved to the edge and looked down over the side. Chucho, foreshortened with perspective, was standing directly below him. His upturned face was pale and anxious, and youthful—he looked like a child of nine or ten. The sidewalk sparkled with mica flecks. Parked cars, haloed sodium vapor lights, water flowing along the gutters of the cambered rain-darkened street.

David straddled the low parapet, lay down briefly, then swung his weight over the side. He dangled there for an instant and then released his grip. Falling, a little off balance, tilting to his right. He hit hard and felt his right ankle turn, heard the popping of muscle and ligament above the slap of his feet hitting the sidewalk. He fell heavily on his right side, lay there for a moment looking up at Chucho's fear-twisted face, then rolled over onto his stomach and slowly stood erect. Now, after the initial stab of pain, the sudden fire, he felt only a prickling numbness in his ankle.

"This way," Chucho said, his voice high, and he began trotting east down the sidewalk.

David followed with a kind of sideways shuffle, favoring his injured ankle, placing the foot flat and flexing his knee to absorb the shock. They passed three staring children, an empty newspaper kiosk, crossed a side street, went another half block, and then turned off into a narrow alley. They paused.

"What happened, man?"

"Ankle."

"Broke it?"

"I don't know."

"Oh, shit, man, we got to move!"

"Let's move then."

He followed Chucho down a maze of dark, smell; alleys where morose dogs and psychopathic cats contended for garbage. Clothes and bedding were hung on overhead electrical wires, and the dresses, sheets, shirts, and trousers were pale levitant-ghosts twitching in the rain. Some distance away, behind him, he heard the hysterical wailing of a klaxon.

They emerged onto a cobblestone street. A taxi engine running, was waiting.

"Get in," Chucho said.

David opened the door and crawled into the back seat. Then Chucho was sitting next to him. The door slammed. The taxi pulled away from the curb.

"Get your head down, man."

David slid low on the seat.

"This here is my uncle," Chucho said.

The driver was a bald, wheezing man who smelled of anise. There were religious medallions hanging from the rearview mirror and luminous plastic statues on the dashboard.

"Hurt bad?"

"Yeah, it's starting to."

"Bad luck, man."

"We've made it this far . . ."

"Sure, we're gonna be okay."

"I don't want to go back there."

"Don't you worry, Flaco, you ain't never going back to that jail."

"I don't know how you did it."

"I oiled the moving parts, man."

The car radio crackled with static and then the dispatcher instructed car 301 to proceed to the Hotel Imperial.

"David sat up. "Isn't this 301?"

"Stay cool, man. We're almost there."

The driver spoke briefly into the microphone. They were now in a section of town that David did not know: dirt roads turned muddy in the rain, few street lights, faded pastel-colored buildings. The taxi turned a corner and coasted halfway down the block.

"Okay," Chucho said. "Out."

David placed most of his weight on his left leg; his right ankle ached now, there was a living core of pain in the center of the prickly numbness. On both sides of the mud street there were block-long adobe walls studded with doors and iron-grilled windows.

"Come on." Chucho walked a few paces, got a key from his pocket, and unlocked a door that was twice as tall as he. David followed him down a short, arched hallway and into a patio where flowering plants twitched and shivered in the rain. Raindrops as big as nickels jumped off the tiles.

David hopped along the patio wall, past a kitchen where women of four generations peered out at him, past a laundry room, two bedrooms, and then through a door on the far wall.

"This here is my room."

It was very small, with just enough space for a single bed, a low table, one chair, and a cheap cardboard wardrobe. There was a stack of comic books on the floor in the corner. A large crucifix was pinned to the wall above the bed; the cross itself was wood, the figure of Christ plastic. Elsewhere on the walls were four unframed woodcuts, apparently torn from a magazine, of Benito Juárez, Emiliano Zapata, Abraham Lincoln, and John F. Kennedy.

David sat on the edge of the bed, rested that way for a time, then swung his feet up and lay back.

"Hurts, huh?" Chucho said.

"Yeah."

"You don't look so good, man. Your face is white."

"Is this your family's house?"

"Naw, man, my people live in a tin hut. I pay rent for this."

"You look like a drowned rat, kid."

"Hey, you look like one drowned gringo rat."

"Even Vigil can add one and one," David said. "He'll figure things out and start looking for you."

"I know."

"Maybe I shouldn't have let you get involved in this mess. Now you're in trouble."

"I was gonna leave this town anyway, man. I'm getting too big for this place."

David started to sit up, became dizzy and lay back again. "Take off my right shoe and sock, will you?"

Chucho sat on the edge of the bed. He unlaced the tennis shoe and then began pulling down on the heel.

"Easy."

"I got to pull it, man."

"Okay. Easy. Easy!"

"It's off. Why don't I cut this sock off, man, instead of pulling."

"All right."

Chucho got out his knife, cut the sock down to the instep, peeled it off and threw it into the corner. "Looks bad. It's big as a melon, Flaco. It's purple."

"That's the way it feels."

There was a light rapping on the door; it opened and Chucho's uncle, the bald taxi driver, entered the room.

"Are we going now?" David asked.

"No, I got to go out and look and listen first. My uncle and me, we got to go around and see what's happening out there."

"Okay."

Chucho patted him on the arm. "If you need anything, man, just yell. These are good people and they give you anything you need, anything."

They left then. The ceiling light was turned off and the door left half open.

SIXTEEN

The Christ on the wall above his head glowed green-blue in the darkness. David listened to the rain for a long time and then he gradually slipped into a state that seemed to exist midway between sleep and consciousness; his visions were too controlled to be dreams, and too silent and pointless to be thoughts.

And then the light was burning and Chucho stood at the end of the bed. His clothes were soaked, his hair a wet cap, and his lips were bluish in the pallor of his face. He shivered; his entire body vibrated with the tremors.

"How does it look?" David asked.

"Bad, 'Mano. The roads are stopped—I never seen so many uniforms, cops and army everyplace."

"I can't stay here."

"No."

"What do you think?"

"I got one idea only."

"Yes?"

"The boat."

David nodded.

"We take the boat away from this place."

"Are the cops after you yet?"

"No. None of them been around asking for me."

"Then you get out of town while you still can. Late tonight I'll sail the skiff down to La Luz. That's only—what?—twenty kilometers. You go there with the money. Have your uncle take you."

"No, I take a bus."

"I'll try to meet you on the beach at La Luz late tonight. Okay? If I don't show up by dawn take the money and run."

Chucho nodded.

"Is your uncle outside?"

"Yeah."

"Good. Let's go and try to find Dr. Pacheco."

"No, man, not Pacheco. He'll get the cops after us."

"Pacheco's a bastard, but not that kind. He's his own kind."

"Hey, what are you talking, Flaco?"

"Trust me."

"I trust you, man, but I don't trust that Pacheco."

David's ankle and swelled and stiffened, and when he lowered his feet to the floor the pain was like a continuous electrical impulse. His ankle *was* swollen to the size of a melon; it was rounded, smooth, and white except for some streaky violet bruises. His ankle bones were buried in the swelling, his lower leg had thickened slightly, and his toes protruded like stubby fingers on a comic balloon.

Chucho helped him through the patio and out onto the street. The air had cooled and smelled faintly of iron. Puddles in the road looked like molten bronze in the taxi's headlights.

Doctor Pacheco was not at his home nor at the country club. They took some back streets to Cinco de Mayo and then south to the clinic. Thin horizontal lines of light shone through the Venetian blinds.

"Someone's here," David said.

"I'll go in," Chucho said.

David closed his eyes and waited.

Chucho returned to the car. He opened the door. "Pacheco's here, man. It's okay, he wants you to come in."

Chucho helped him up the long flagstone walk, through the door and into a large waiting room. Pacheco appeared at the entrance to a corridor. He removed the cigar from his teeth and looked at them with smiling contempt.

"Imbecile," he said. He glanced at David's bare, swollen foot, and then into his eyes. "This way, my angels."

They went down the hallway and into a square, white-painted room that contained a desk, an examination table, and a number of padlocked cabinets.

"Help him up onto the table, kid," Pacheco said. "Hurry, you're dripping effluent onto the floor. All right, get out of here. Return to your sewer."

Chucho winked at David and then left the room.

Pacheco gripped the cigar between his teeth. "Well?"

"You always said that you wouldn't loan me money, but would provide free medical care. Here I am."

"See? Even idle social chat leads to obligation. Duty lies in ambush everywhere."

"My ankle, Paco."

"If you had money you would constitute a hard-working physician's entire practice. As it is . . . "

"Paco, I can't stay long. Sorry . . . Dr. Pacheco."

"Go ahead and call me Paco. None of my friends do." He smiled around his cigar. "Classic bum."

"I'm not really a loser. It just looks that way."

"I know, you're a champion. Well, let me look at your foot."

"Is it broken?"

"May I examine it before I say? Or do you want me to go into a dark room and wait for spiritual assistance in my diagnosis?"

"Sorry."

"I would prefer to rely on my medical training and experience while attempting to determine what is wrong with your fucking ankle."

"Well, examine it, then."

Pain as Dr. Pacheco articulated his foot. He pressed his fingers on the arch.

"Does it hurt there?"

"No."

"Here, on the instep?"

"Some, not too much."

"The Achilles tendon?"

"A twinge, but not bad."

"Here?"

"Yes!"

"And here, around the outside ankle bone?"

"Jesus Christ, Paco!"

Pacheco twisted his big toe. "This little piggy went to market . . . "

"What! What are you doing?"

He twisted the second toe. "This little piggy stayed home . . . "

"Oh! Oh, you son of a bitch!"

"This little piggy had roast beef . . . "

"You're insane!"

Pacheco slid into his field of vision. Cigar smoke streamed from his mouth and nostrils.

"You're crazy. What does Hippocrates say about torture?"

"I don't believe he mentioned it, but I assume he would have considered it an ethically dubious practice."

"What about my ankle?"

"A very bad sprain, I think."

"You think. Maybe you ought to go into that dark room."

"I couldn't say for sure without seeing some pictures."

"Well, take some X rays."

"I am not an X-ray technologist, my friend."

"You're a sadist."

"Lots of doctors are sadists, but most of them sublimate their sadism better than I."

David laughed.

"You are changing, my friend. That isn't bad. I look at you and I don't see my little Bambi anymore."

"Bambi broke out of jail tonight."

"I know. Vigil telephoned me an hour ago. He said that you had escaped and might come to see me."

"I'm here."

"The man is *rabioso*, David. He is a mad dog at this moment. He regards your escape as a gesture, a personal insult. Do you understand?"

David shook his head.

"You've heard of *ley de fuga*? The law of flight? Listen, you cannot surrender tonight. You cannot be captured. They will kill you. Tomorrow—well, perhaps tomorrow it will be different. But if the police see you tonight they'll shoot."

"Will you put a cast on my foot?"

"I told you that I believe it's only a sprain."

"Listen, Paco, I'm going to have to use this foot a lot during the next few days. A cast will give it some support. And if it does happen to be broken . . . "

Pacheco shrugged. "All right. I'll put on a walking cast. And I'll give you some codeine tablets. And that is all."

"It's enough."

"It's too much."

"No, it isn't, not if we're friends."

Pacheco smiled sardonically. "Oh, well, friends . . . Shall we cut open a couple of our veins and bleed into each other to make it official?"

"I don't trust your knowledge of anatomy. You'd probably cut open my artery."

"I should betray you right now. I'm ashamed that you could pollute our relationship with that word. Friends indeed!"

"Paco . . . "

"A cast isn't the best idea right now. The swelling should be reduced first."

"I'm running out of time."

"Okay. It's your foot."

The cast was bulky, heavy, with a rubber disk set into the bottom. While the plaster was setting, Pacheco brought a bottle of cognac and two glasses over to the examination table.

"Say 'when,' " Pacheco said, pouring.

"When."

"That was a delayed 'when.' Don't take any of the codeine for a while."

"All right."

"You know, don't you, that I am going to telephone Vigil five minutes after you leave here."

"Ten minutes?"

"Yes, ten minutes, maybe fifteen. And I am going to tell him that you physically intimidated me, forced me to put a cast on your right foot. I want to explain that cast *before* they carry your remains into the basement of the hospital."

"Don't tell Vigil that Chucho was with me."

"I'll misdirect the fool. I'll tell him that you intend to hide out in the mangrove swamp."

"Christ, no, don't tell him that. I may go there tonight."

"I'll say that you intend to hike overland to the coastal highway."

"That's all right."

Pacheco bit the tip off of a fresh cigar. "You are a jackass, a—I almost said a romantic jackass, but that's redundant. A daring escape from jail, now a fugitive from the police of two nations."

"One nation—Vigil told me that I'm clear in the States now."

"Do you regard yourself as a gallant character, David?"

"Hardly."

"Jackass! You should have remained in jail. There is only one healthy way out of Mexican jails, and that is through the front door."

"I didn't kill the girl, Paco."

Pacheco slowly rotated the end of his cigar in a match flame; then he dropped that match and lit the cigar with another.

"I didn't do it."

"Maybe so. Maybe the kid killed her."

"Chucho?"

"He used to follow her around."

"How do you know that?"

"She told me. It worried her. She said the kid hadn't approached her, but he was always around, always here, at the beach when she went swimming, at the market when she shopped, waiting outside of her hotel, sitting a few seats behind her at the movie theater."

"How did you happen to know her, Paco?"

"I was treating her for gonorrhea. She was another of my American charity patients. Incidentally, have you noticed a burning sensation when you urinate? Do you have the dribbles, David?"

"Go on, Paco."

"She came here to the clinic one night. She'd lost the oral antibiotic capsules that I had given her. I gave her some more and she told me about the kid, that he had followed her here and she was afraid to walk back to her hotel. I gave her a ride. The kid was in a doorway across the street when we left."

David shook his head. "Chucho might follow her, Paco, he probably did. Maybe he was in love. But he didn't murder her."

"What else could you say with your wonderfully sentimental view of human nature? Little Jesús is—what's the word?—your friend." He nodded. "Your lover for all I know."

David smiled. "Dr. Pacheco, little Jesús told me that he is sure that you killed the girl."

Pacheco tapped the cast with his knuckles. "On your way, derelict."

David sat up and swung his feet over the table edge. He closed his eyes for half a minute as blood throbbed in his ankle, and then he carefully stepped down. After a few paces the pain seemed to diminish.

"Paco, what do you do here alone late at night?"

"I experiment with my collection of cadavers. I try an arm here, a leg there, a head somewhere near the top. If you'll hang around until midnight I'll endeavor to transplant your puny brain into Boris's magnificent physique."

"Seriously."

They paused by the door.

Pacheco squinted through the cigar smoke. "I tell you this only because it is none of your business. I am engaged in writing an abstruse, nearly incomprehensible philosophical tome. I have five hundred pages. I have at least that far to go. My philosophical doctrine will be known through the ages as Pachecismo, or nihilism without consolation. It will not be contaminated by gods, morality, ethics, pity, beauty, or hope. It will be true. No one will read it."

"I will. I'll read it when it comes out in the condensed Reader's Digest version."

Pacheco laughed. "You are more than a little sadistic yourself. Get out of here. You'll be dead within six hours. I'll do the autopsy and save your liver for my cat."

Back in the taxi, David said that he wanted to be dropped off at the base of the *Avenida de las Americas*.

"What're you gonna do, man?"

"Go up to Harry's place."

"That's crazy. You're crazy, 'Mano. I don't want nothing to do with you anymore."

"I want to have a little talk with Ruben. I think he's the one who killed the girl."

"Okay, man, okay. I meet you at La Luz if you make it there. But I don't get you out of jail again."

SEVENTEEN

David slowly climbed the *Avenida de las Americas*, a great coiled snake of a road that penetrated the hills behind town where the wealthy lived. Cocktail heaven, Chucho called the area. The road changed from dirt to asphalt at some invisible line dividing castes. You could suddenly see money and power: the road was now paved; there were yellow sodium vapor lamps; frequent police and private security patrols; meticulously pruned trees and shrubbery. Narrow side roads ascended into the darkness and high above seemed to explode like Fourth of July rockets into sprays of colored lights. "I wish I had money to live like that, 'Mano," Chucho had once said. "So I could decide myself not to live like that."

All of the estates he passed were surrounded by ivy-covered walls, and there were wrought-iron gates, barking dogs, spotlights mounted in trees, broken glass embedded atop the walls glinting amber and green and silver in the lights—the menace of defense. David stayed as much as possible to the shadows, away from the lights and cruising cops and killer dogs.

His foot aching, he paused to rest on the middle loop of a large S turn. Far below he could see the grid of village lights; and below and beyond the town there was a long expanse of darkness which suddenly erupted into flashing lines of surf. Even this high he could hear the remote inhalations and exhalations of the sea.

David went on. He now felt the just-right combination of anxiety and lucidity: not too hot and not too cold emotionally, the past inert and the future only possibility with himself poised in the volatile present. Seconds ticked away like tiny bombs; the detonations drummed in his ears. Each concussive moment possessed an incomparable design, like a snowflake or crystal, a subtle elegance that had not existed before and would never be duplicated. It didn't matter that he was a fugitive with an unlucky past and a perilous future; it was enough for now to climb this hill, sweating, in pain, while ferocious dogs snarled and barked behind the high stone walls.

A side road angled off toward the Villa Flores, Rudd's place. The house and grounds were blazing with lights, the sky above glowed, and David could hear the swooning sentimental strings of Tchaikovsky's *Pathetique.*

David was just a few yards from the wall when two small shadows melted free of a larger shadow and came toward him in a swift, predatory rush. Low to the ground, snuffling softly, bounding, they came directly toward him and then at the last instant, recognizing his scent, they broke aside. Harry's Doberman pinschers,

Rasputin and Torquemada. They knew him. They were
not friendly, they remained stiff and suspicious, but they
did not attack.

David went on down the gravel driveway to the
patio gate. It was a heavy wrought-iron structure with
sharp, outward curving spikes at the top, secured with a
thick coil of chain—each link as big as a donut—and a
massive steel padlock.

He looked through the grille. Every window in the
house, the guest house, and the servants' quarters glowed
brightly. The tennis court was lit, each bulb encircled by
a fluttering halo of moths; the pool and the terrace were
lit too; and even the strings of colored Chinese lanterns,
left up since the party, were burning.

David could smell insecticide, and chlorine from
the pool, and hear the bathetic, melodic theme of the
Pathetique. The phonograph was connected to a number of speakers scattered around the grounds and music
surrounded him, issued from flower-laden shrubs and
trees, seemed to materialize out of the air.

He moved twenty paces to the pedestrian gate. He
could see the entire pool area from here: the checker-
board of blue and white tiles, the sagging strings of colored lights, the wrinkled water and its reflected tars. It
was all tinctured by the vibrating emerald glow of the
pool. Now David briefly thought about the party: a bad
party, an evil mood, cannibals in silk.

And then he saw Harry sitting alone at a small
round table on the far side of the pool, on a too-small
chair that looked like lace. Nearby was a wheeled drink

caddy. There was a drink on the table in front of Harry, cigarettes and a lighter, and a revolver.

The *Pathetique* ended, there was a moment of silence, and then David heard the first chords of Bach's *Jesu, Joy of Man's Desiring.*

Harry, wearing slacks and a loose sport shirt, looked disheveled, as if he had napped while clothed, and his thinning, brindle hair was whorled and horned. He sipped his drink. Cracked his knuckles. Rocked in the hair. Expanded his barrel chest with air, held it for a time, slowly let it deflate. He had a stocky, powerful body, but even so his head appeared disproportionately large; big, crudely chiseled features, globular temples, jaw curved like the end of a spade.

Now Harry smiled at something, shook his head, tilted the chair forward, and picked up the revolver. It was a big handgun that looked heavily awkward even in Harry's meaty hand. The thumb seemed to detach itself from the hand, lifted and curved to cock the hammer. Cocked, the black steel, that dark oily machine, became a different thing, almost lithe and alive. It acquired a certain grace. Harry pressed the muzzle against his temple.

"No," David said. What had been intended to be a shout emerged as a whisper.

Rudd sat erect in the chair, his left hand palm-down on the table, his right arm crooked at the elbow, with the revolver's barrel fashioning a conduit into his brain, linking the two incompatible worlds.

"No, Harry." Softly, another whisper.

And then Harry Rudd somehow diminished. He held the same position, but he looked smaller now, almost frail, and David was not surprised when he uncocked the revolver and replaced it on the table. He sipped his drink left-handed, shook a cigarette out of the package and lit it, snorted smoke through his nostrils. Then was something ironic about his expression now; he was not smiling, but he looked as though he might smile at any second.

David waited for a couple of minutes, watching, and then he said, "Harry."

Rudd glanced toward the house.

"Over here. At the gate."

Rudd lowered his head and stared.

"It's me, David."

He was silent for a time and then he said, "Been expecting you, kid. The gate's not locked. Come on in."

David lifted the latch, passed through, closed the gate, and limped around the pool apron.

"How long have you been there?"

"I just now got here."

"I didn't hear the dogs."

"They know me."

"At night those dogs aren't supposed to know anybody but me and my wife."

"What's the gun for, Harry?"

"Sit down. Make yourself a drink."

David sat across from Harry and pulled the drink caddy over. Bottles and glasses, shakers, siphons, cut fruit, a big silver ice bucket, slender implements that looked like surgical tools. David mixed a daiquiri on ice.

"Old Dave Daiquiri," Harry said. "We bushwhacked them, didn't we, kid?"

"We did that, all right." David took a cigarette from the package on the table, lit it, inhaled.

"Vigil called. You're hot, Dave, really hot."

"I know."

"What happened to your foot?"

"I sprained it coming over the wall."

"What are you doing here?"

"Thought I'd say hello. And good-bye."

"How long were you standing out there watching me?"

"I just arrived, Harry. I walked up to the gate and called to you."

"You're on fire, lad. I don't think the Mexican cops are going to take you in this time."

"Where is everyone?"

"Norma is still in the States. I sent the servants away."

"Why are all the lights on, Harry? What is the gun for?"

"Prowlers have been coming around here lately. I hear them out there at night, howling obscenities. They were bold enough to come into the house last night, but I heard them and went downstairs and they scattered like roaches."

David sipped his drink, drew on the cigarette.

"You don't believe me?"

"But Harry, the music, sitting here in all of these lights . . . "

"I'm not going to *hide*," he said. "I've never hidden in my life and it's too late to start now. I'll sit in the open, in the lights—let them come. They're invited."

"Harry . . . "

"Paranoid, huh? Think old Harry's cracked up, do you kid?"

"You aren't crazy. Harry. But you're under terrific pressure."

"No hokum, Dave, none of that."

"Am I the one you're waiting for?"

"I said no hokum, no twist-around, turn-around, hoity-freudy chitchat."

"Poor Harry," David said. "All of these walls with broken glass on top, spiked gates, floodlights and attack dogs, guns—and what we've got to fear most is in our own hearts. Right, Harry?"

"No pop songs, no bittersweet lyrics. Let's stay close to what's real or we'll get lost."

David drained his glass, shifted sideways to mix another drink, turned back again.

"Are you drunk, Harry?"

"I am within my capacity."

"You know, for a while I half thought that Dr. Pacheco had killed the girl. I had information that made me think that he was at least laying her."

"Pacheco would screw the Christmas turkey. Then say grace."

"But I don't see it that way anymore."

"Naw, it wasn't Paco. He does his killing in the OR."

"And then, Harry, I figured that it just might be the kid, Chucho Aguilar."

"Now that is a possibility."

"No. It wasn't Chucho. But then tonight I wondered—Ruben?"

"Ah, but then you decided that it wasn't Ruben either, didn't you, Dave Daiquiri?"

"That's right."

"You concluded that it was your old pal and mentor, Harold T-for-Tipton Rudd."

"Yeah."

All along the revolver had been a silent third member at the table. It looked as though it had been roughly hewn out of a block of steel and not quite completed, unsmoothed and unpolished; it did not have the sleek, sinister grace of so many weapons.

"That's a huge gun," David said. "What is it?"

"A .44 Magnum."

"Is that the one that'll put a slug through the engine block of a car?"

"Something like that."

"Overkill."

"No such thing. Dead is dead."

"If a man put that barrel up against his temple . . . "

Rudd stared at David for a time and then he smiled faintly. "You were out there longer than you said."

"Yes."

"I was only clowning around."

"Sure, Harry."

"Why didn't you try to stop me?"

"I said something."

"I didn't hear."

"It came out a whisper."

Rudd smiled and nodded.

"It would have been like shouting at a wake."

"Very funny."

"I wasn't trying to be funny. What I mean, Harry, is that there is something awesome and intimidating about watching a man attempt suicide. That isn't a small decision, it maybe deserves respect, and I wasn't sure that I had the right to interfere."

"Well, David, there is no doubt some truth in that, but I was squeezing that trigger as hard as I could, if you understand what I mean, and I might have appreciated hearing a concerned voice."

"Sorry."

The Bach record was the last of the stack; when it ended there was only a long, scratchy silence.

Then Harry said: "I tried it last night too. I'm a strong man, but I wasn't strong enough to pull the trigger."

"Are you going to try again?"

He shrugged. "I don't know. That isn't something you can make resolutions about. How can you know? But it's funny, kid, everything started looking so cheap. A dime-store world. Dime-store dummies instead of people. Sleaze, real sleaze. I always enjoyed vulgarity, it was my element, it made me happier than a pig in mud. But now it gets me sick. It's hard to take, this slimy world."

"Did it start looking that way after you killed the girl?"

"No, before, it started long before. But maybe it all came to a head then, all the poison concentrated. And it was an accident, Dave, Jesus Christ, man, it was no more murder than if she'd fallen down the stairs in my house or drowned in my pool."

"She was raped, Harry. She was strangled. She was thrown down on the rocks."

"You knew it was me, huh?"

"Not until I came here tonight and saw the gun up against your head."

"That proves nothing."

"It demonstrates remorse."

"Remorse. Remorse is what you show to the judge. Contrite is the absolute tops you can expect from folks. Remorse was invented by theologians looking for revenge in the here and now. Ain't no such thing. Only neurotics believe in remorse, guilt, like that."

"I'll take your word for it. You were the one with a gun against your head."

Rudd smiled wryly. "I'm just tired, babe. Really tired."

"Do you want to tell me about it, Harry?"

"I guess so. Sure, why not? I guess I should tell someone."

EIGHTEEN

It happened, Harry said, because of a couple of trivial humiliations.

He had spent most of that evening in the lounge of the Hotel El Presidente, drinking and playing liar's poker with a couple of his pals. They had gambled with one-hundred-peso notes and Harry had lost about forty dollars. Not much money, but enough to sour his mood a little; he had never learned how to accept losing, hated it, regarded it as a little death—every time you lost, whether a dime or an argument or what the Asians call face, a chip was taken out of your self-esteem and you entered the next contest with that much less confidence. Losing was an accumulative poison like lead or arsenic; small doses did not appear to cause much harm, but they collected and in time . . .

Later two American women had come into the lounge, school teachers down from St. Paul, all dressed up and smelling like crushed flowers. Pretty enough. Blue eyelids at half mast as they languorously sipped their margaritas and evaluated the bodies in the room.

No wedding rings though they were married, all right, you could tell. A pair of Spanish teachers on a four-day vacation, here to explore some carnal aspects of Mexican culture. The women were much younger than Harry, but not kids; early thirties, maybe thirty-two or -three.

If Harry hadn't been drunk and feeling somewhat aggressive over losing the forty dollars ("The loss remember, not the cash"), he would have known better than to approach those women. They hadn't come all this way, then got themselves bathed and oiled and perfumed in order to make love to a couple of paunchy middle-aged men; they were looking for physical sensation, a pair of healthy young animals, Mexican he-goats. And aside from that, those two would never have accepted Harry's rough courting ways, his loud good humor and vulgar intimacy. Harry was successful with a certain type of woman, even a young one from time to time; but the teachers were basically genteel types, aspirants to the middle class, who had taken off on a long weekend of discriminate whoring. They would again be respectable, probably demure, when back home. Harry was simply not their meat, and he knew it before he and Ted Keyes approached the table. It was a kind of challenge. But a sucker's game—he had no chance of winning.

The women were coolly polite. They answered questions. They parted their lips in frozen smiles. But they would not accept a drink and did not invite them to sit down. Ted acted like a fourteen-year-old boy, shy and smirky, feeling evil. It became embarrassing. The girls were not the kind to be overtly rude. Better if they were. But they were rude in their postures and flat voices and exchanged glances and silences. And Harry started feeling grossly huge and hairy and loud. But he couldn't stop. And for the first time in many years he felt ashamed of his peasant's body, his thick arms and hands, his gravelly voice, the crudity he had enjoyed flourishing like a cudgel. He kept up his flippant chatter but he was beginning to sweat now. And it went on and on, getting worse. Ted surrendered and returned to the bar. But he, jackass Harry, went on trying to charm a couple of dry bitches from Minnesota. Those dumb suburban tramps, those empty classroom fascists, were making Harry Rudd look like a nothing. They turned and raised their eyebrows at people at adjoining tables, humorously implicating them in their plight—what can we do with this clumsy buffalo? And Harry couldn't stop talking, couldn't turn off his rictus smile. He heard a whine in his voice, an abject note. He was begging them to be kind! Now, after all of these years, in a plastic hotel lounge in front of forty plastic, make-believe people, he, the Harry Tipton Rudd that he'd constructed like a fortress, was falling apart. Jesus Christ, he'd built himself to last. To stay the full course. And now, ten years, fifteen years too soon, he was undergoing a petty and humiliating public crackup.

He left the bar finally, the band drummer sending him off with a snare roll.

He knew that he should go home, eat something, rest, organize his thinking, but he couldn't; he was impelled to return to the arena and attempt to salvage something—

pride—from this night. He went to another bar, had a drink, met a couple of surfers down from Long Beach who beat him for twelve dollars rolling dice. And one of the goddamned kids beat him arm wrestling. Harry had not lost an arm-wrestling match in thirty years. That long. He was pretty drunk by now and got mad over something or other and challenged the kid to a fight, but the guy just laughed and teased and put him off. What it was, the kid was too decent to fight a drunken old man. And Harry was further shamed because he'd felt relieved when the surfer refused to fight him. He was an ox, bigger than Harry by six inches and twenty-five pounds, and younger by at least thirty years.

This was the first time since Harry was eighteen that he had met a man and realized that he would be unable to beat him in a fair fight. There were men who could have whipped him, of course, plenty of them, but Harry had never admitted it. He did now, and it hurt. Damn, it hurt! There would be many more similar hurts in the future. And he figured that if he wasn't certain that in the last resort he could not whip a man then he was at a disadvantage. You didn't have to play the Neanderthal; but if you knew and others knew that violence was your down card, you got concessions. People were easily intimidated, usually without being aware of it. Harry knew that for some time he would be able to command respect, but the years of deference were ending. And soon, much too soon, when time had plundered his strength, even the naturally servile—the punks and creeps—would be able to treat him with insolence.

He left the bar, ate a roasted ear of corn at a sidewalk cart, then went to his car.

He was losing power. His great vitality was swiftly diminishing. On the wrong side of fifty now. He slept ten hours a day, he got tired after one set of hard tennis, a night of serious boozing could screw him up for four days, his lust far exceeded his performance, doctors frowned and talked about more tests. Each morning he awakened with the knowledge that another spadeful of dirt had been excavated from his grave.

Harry drove away in his car. He rolled down the windows and let the hot air blast in. Through town and out onto the cliff road. Good, clean, hot wind drying his sweat, headlights carving a bright tunnel out of darkness. Going a little too fast for the road, red-lining it. You didn't have to submit to slow decay; a sharp twist of the steering wheel . . .

He braked lightly for a curve, down-shifted twice, then accelerated and went up through the gears. Ahead, he saw the figure of the girl in the headlights. She was walking down the right shoulder. You knew who it was even at three hundred yards—she was the only Arab in town.

Harry hit the brakes, stopped well beyond her, put the car into reverse, and backed up.

"Where are you going?"

A lost, fragile thing, this goofy moonchild. Shaking her head. Trying to speak and failing.

Crazy child weeping out of gratitude or fear or a private anguish or simple-minded happiness—how could you tell? She opened the door and got in.

"Where to?" Harry asked.

"Home," she sobbed. "The stars."

Harry drove away, thinking of sex, uncomplicated, curative sex. This girl was young and not unattractive, and her mind was blasted; he would use her body, heal himself in it, triumph.

He turned the car off onto a large, wedge-shaped plateau overlooking the sea. Down below the lines of hissing surf; above the stars—her home.

He got a blanket out of the trunk of his car and spread it over the ground.

"I raped her."

That was all, Harry raped her, knowing that he could have easily seduced her. She writhed and screamed. Of course. It was okay at first; that was even a part of what he was looking for. But she continued to fight, and she screamed—"God, you have never heard such screaming"—and Harry hit her. That was maybe part of it too, hitting her. But it didn't end. And so to silence her he placed his hands around her throat. And it crackled faintly. But there was no intent, there was never any *intent* to kill her. It was almost like a kind of game; it had seemed that she wasn't real, not quite wholly human.

"I cried when I realized that she was dead. It was so . . . useless. Futile. What was the point? She didn't understand me, my intentions. There was just this crackling noise in her throat. It was so easy. I didn't use any more strength than . . . What could I do afterwards? There was nothing I could do."

"There's one thing you can do, Harry," David said. "You can get me off the hook."

"No," Rudd said. "No, I'm not going to ruin my life for those three or four minutes. No, kid, I lived decently fifty-one years, as me, I'm not going to ruin all of that for three minutes of dream."

"It was you, Harry."

"No."

"You did it."

"No, Harry Rudd made a few bucks, had some laughs, was rough and tough, but he never did anything like that. No one can judge an entire lifetime on what a pair of strong hands did in a few seconds. It was a freak accident, nothing more, and you know goddamned well that it wasn't Harry who did it."

"It *was* Harry, it was you."

"Are you for me, kid, or against me?"

"I just want you to see the truth."

"Identify your alliance."

"The truth, Harry. You killed her."

"The truth is that Harry was a good guy for fifty-one years, hurt no one seriously. He met a payroll, raised a fine family, was a fairly good man. He was a bad man for a few minutes. Is it fair that he should be punished for that one lapse?"

"I don't know about that, Harry. But is it fair that you make me suffer for those few minutes? Why should I have to pay for your lapse?"

"Davey, you got a bad bounce, that's all. What can I tell you? All I can say is that it's your bounce and you've got to field the ball as best as you can."

"Harry, Christ, man, you're talking about bad bounces and I'm talking about my life. You talked to Vigil about me, you made me poison. You put that veil in my room after the tennis match, you phoned the cops and—"

"I'm sorry. I panicked, that's all. I'd do it differently now."

"Why *me*, Harry?"

"Because they figured it was you."

"But *me*—weren't we friends?"

"I just panicked, kid. I'm sorry. You can't know how sorry I am. Do you think it doesn't half kill me to know that I did that to you? God, boy, I have some sense of honor and loyalty. But I got scared, all I could think about was saving myself and my family."

"It was wrong."

"You don't have a wife and kids, grandkids, a reputation that took fifty-one years to build."

"All right."

"It won't necessarily destroy *your* life."

"Of course it will."

"They don't have the death penalty in this country."

David smiled.

"You're young, without obligations—you can absorb something like this."

"Sure."

"But if they got me—Dave, it wouldn't be just my life that's ruined, I got a wife, children, grandchildren, friends."

"Give me some money."

"What?"

"Give me some money so that I can try to get out of this country."

"Hey, yeah, now you're thinking, kid. I don't know what was wrong with me, I should have thought of it. Christ, yes! Wait right here. Don't go away. I want to help. I did a bad thing to you, Davey, and I want to help as much as I can."

Harry stood up, nodded at David, then turned and hurriedly walked along the pool apron toward the house.

David started to mix another drink and then stopped; he was already a little high, not drunk but bolder and freer than he had any right to be. Stupid. He had been putting pressure on Harry and the man simply could not handle any more; already he was talking about himself in the third person and sticking a gun barrel against his temple.

The phonograph was silent. David could hear the flutter of moth wings and the sucking of the pool drains and the remote yapping of a dog. He closed his eyes and saw parachute-shaped retinal lights float obliquely through the darkness. The air smelled of delicious poisons.

He turned and looked toward the house. Harry, framed in the light of an upstairs window, was staring at him. They were about sixty feet apart. Harry was still; he did not respond to David's languid wave. They stared at each other for a time and then Harry slipped out of sight.

David picked up the revolver, swung out the cylinder, and quickly removed the bullets. He tossed them underhand into the pool, closed the cylinder, and replaced the gun on the table.

NINETEEN

A little later David heard a muffled voice droning in the house and then, still talking, Harry shouldered his way through the screen door. He carried a covered dish in one hand and half a loaf of bread in the other. The door slammed behind him, banging twice, and Harry walked swiftly down alongside the pool, talking in an agitated way. ". . . don't keep much money in the house . . . thieves . . . take what I have and welcome to it . . . so sorry . . . some food here, you must be starving."

He set the dish and bread on the table, then emptied his pockets; a wad of dirty peso notes in various colors, five crisp one-hundred-dollar bills, and a handful of jewelry—rings, a bracelet, pearl earrings, a pearl choker.

"Harry, what the hell . . . "

"There's only about eight hundred dollars there in cash, all I had in my pocket and in the house. But here's some of Norma's jewelry, not her best stuff, that's in the bank, but this is okay, it's real, you can sell it or pawn it and get a fair amount of money."

"I don't want your wife's jewelry."

"Christ, man, take it! It's the least I can do. Norma won't miss this stuff much. I'll replace it for her."

David shook his head.

"Take it."

David folded the money and stuffed it into his trouser pocket.

"The jewelry, too."

"No."

"Take it. For me, as a favor to me. You'll need money. And when you get safe in the States write me and I'll send you a check, a big check. Now please, take the jewelry."

David scooped up the jewelry and put it in his other pocket.

"Now look, eat something. Do you want a beer with that?"

"No."

"Sure you do, I'll get you a cold one." Harry turned and started toward the house in a near trot.

There was half of a cold barbecued chicken in the dish. David pulled off the leg and began eating. This eager-to-please Harry Rudd worried him more than the guilty, suicidal Harry. He'd halfway trusted the man who had held a revolver to his temple for thirty seconds; that Harry, believing himself to be alone, had been emotionally sincere. He'd been acting out of deep impulse. He'd been obeying a certain inner logic. David had not feared him. But he was not convinced by this anxious Harry, the shy and sensitive Harry who gushed and served him food and made an extra trip to the house for beer, gave him money and his wife's jewelry. That was a lie. And David didn't like the way Harry had stared out the window at him for so long, as if coolly watching the approach of a storm.

Now Harry was on his way back with two cans of beer, saying, ". . . make a lousy bachelor, wish Norma would get back. The servants, anyway, listen to her."

David accepted the beer, opened one and drank deeply.

Harry sat down. "Jesus, I miss Norma, I really do. She could have helped me through this. By just being here, I mean. By being Norma and being at my side. It never would have *happened* if she . . . "

David peeled some of the white breast meat off of the chicken. "What's funny, Harry, is how sanctimonious you were after the tennis match, talking about my brutality, and then later in the jail."

"Yeah, well, I felt that way. Both times. Look, kid, I don't go around thinking of myself as a murderer."

"And then, at the jail, you cried."

"I've been very emotional lately. You can understand that."

"Sure. Harry, I've got to use your bathroom."

"Hell, there's no one around, water the shrubbery."

"I'll fertilize the shrubbery if you say so."

He smiled. "You know where the cans are."

David stood up, drained his beer, and started for the house.

"Turn off some of these lights," Harry said. "You know where the switch box is."

David waved without turning around. He could clearly see the bullets in the shallow end of the pool. He went in past the pool and high dive platform, up the steps, and through the screen door into the house. The living room was a mess; wife gone, servants gone, Harry a slob.

Each lever in the bank of levers was identified with printing on strips of tape; he turned off the tennis court lights, the terrace and patio lights, the Chinese lanterns, and the floodlights outside the walls.

Let old Harry believe that everything was going smoothly, no panic, plenty of time to do this right, in the dark, bang.

Burglar shot to death. Loot found in pockets. Suspected rapist-murderer and jail escapee, David Rhodes, was last night shot by . . . Sure, Harry.

David stuffed the money and jewelry beneath one of the sofas, got up and walked to the window, carefully eased back the drape, and looked out. Harry was standing now, looking down into the shallow end of the pool, his figure was mottled bluish with pool light; oblong rings quivered over his face and torso. He appeared dejected rather than angry; knees slightly bent, hands hanging at his sides (one holding that huge gun), head lowered.

Back door, the kitchen. David limped hurriedly through the living room, the long dining room, and into the kitchen. He pulled out half a dozen drawers, found the cutlery in a mahogany box, and removed the butcher knife. It was heavy, with a smooth wooden handle, a dagger point, and a blade that had been discolored almost black except for the honed edge—good carbon steel.

The back door was locked, bolted, and had a safety chain. The bolt and the chain were easy but how did you work this huge bitch of a lock?

He heard the screen door slam shut. "Dave? David? Where are you, son?"

A long silence and then Harry was moving heavily up the staircase, calling, "Dave, are you in the upstairs can? Listen, why did you empty my gun? I'm not going to hurt myself. I'm over that now. You've helped me by understanding."

David fumbled with the lock, cursing softly, finally got it open and slipped out into the rear garden. House lights, upstairs and down, spread yellow, crosshatched rectangles of light over the ground. Here and there, as if deliberately spotlighted, were large scarlet and gold trumpets, lime and jacaranda trees, jasmine, bougainvillea, a trellis crawling with ivy, a pool which he knew contained orange carp, and a dozen yards of flagstone walk that vanished into darkness near the wall.

He moved slowly, staying as much as possible to the shadows. From beyond the wall he could hear the chirruping of crickets and frogs and, far off, the doleful vibrato fluting of an owl.

Then, caught in a band of light, he heard a persistent tapping noise, turned, and looked up over his right shoulder. Harry, standing before an upstairs window, was clicking the muzzle of his revolver against the glass.

He slowly lowered the gun and stared down at David. His expression had changed; his features were rigid now, set in a kind of malign rictus. Eyes flat; mouth almost smug. Massive, still, shadowed, and foreshortened, he reminded David of the old stone sculptures he had seen in museums, stylized representations of some merciless deity who was both bloodthirsty and serene, mad yet capable. The same sculptures which had coldly stared down upon bloody, unimaginable scenes of human sacrifice.

David passed through the gate and limped down a winding path through the woods. There were deciduous trees and conifers here, and palms and cactus, ferns, sword grass, and hanging masses of parasitic moss. The moon was high now, and fractured pieces of light and shadow cast complex mosaics over the ground. The mosaics shifted kaleidoscopically as wind blew through the interstices of branches overhead.

He came to a fork in the path, chose the right which led more steeply downhill. Paths meandered all over these hills; they were used mostly by children, and servants taking shortcuts to work from the town below.

When his eyes adjusted to the darkness he began jogging down the trail, his injured leg stiff, his left pushing off, flexing, absorbing most of the shock. He was not aware of the pain in his ankle now. He wanted to move as swiftly as he could without submitting to panic.

The path curved into a small terraced clearing that had been planted with tomatoes and corn and beans. Moonlight filmed the air and etched the leaves with delicate filigree. White stones lined the edge of each terrace. A wall of darkness surrounded the clearing.

He stopped, cocked his head, and listened. His breathing and the metronomic clicking of crickets and the faint, underlying whine of silence itself. Then he heard the barking of a dog. A car horn far below in town. And then the high tree branches clattered in a gust of wind, leaves spun and rattled, flashing light, and on the wind he could smell earth and decay and the sea. The wind died. He could feel each heartbeat in his ankle. His heart jumped in his chest and an instant later his ankle throbbed. He wiped the burning sweat out of his eyes and heard the ticking of his watch. Ticking watch, ticking crickets, ticking heart, ticking night. Stars flickered against the black dial of the sky. Tick-tock, tonight you die.

And then, above and well to the north, he heard brush crackling. Not loud, not close. Think.

He limped down the path to the edge of the clearing and then turned off into the woods. Blackness flecked with angular fragments of moonlight, a thick tangle of underbrush—thorny coils and whips, calf-high sword grass, bristling cactus. He flushed a bird which whistled piercingly and beat away toward the sky.

He stopped, sat on the ground with his back against a palm. Insects buzzed like static in the deep silence. There were many small cuts on his arms and face. His clothes were soaked with sweat. It was not the clear sweat you got from sport or physical labor; this smelled of fear and sickness.

He commanded himself to remain here. He knew that if he kept his head, did not panic, he would be all right. It was not just a choice of flight or fight; there was this third alternative, hide. That was the hardest but the best. Harry could pass within three yards and not see him.

There was a noise outside the thicket. Breathing, a kind of snuffling sound. He tightened his grip on the knife handle.

The brush rustled, parted briefly, and admitted a shadow. Another shadow followed. Quick, springy shapes, simultaneously wary and eager.

The dogs, the goddamned dogs, he had forgotten about them! They stood nearby, motionless now on still legs, cautiously sniffing the air. One of them growled far back in its throat, rumbled. Rasputin, probably, the more aggressive of the two. Rasputin and Torquemada. Oh, my God! And Harry coming down through the darkness.

David got up and crashed blindly through the brush to the clearing. Still empty, coldly limned with moonlight. He hesitated for a moment, paralyzed, then turned and started down the path. Far ahead the lights of a house. Below, other lights, other houses, and the galaxy of town lights. He stumbled, partly recovered and staggered on a few paces, turned a corner, and fell heavily. The dogs were on him immediately. Growls, hot breath, the musty, furry, slightly rotten canine smell.

He got up, resumed running. The dogs stayed with him, bounding alongside, ranging ahead and falling back, growling. The longer he ran the wilder the dogs became. They were excited by the chase; a game was rapidly turning into a primal reflex. They could smell his blood and fear-sweat, were aware that he ran with an unnatural motion. A big wounded mammal loping terror-stricken through the night forest. A few minutes ago they had been pets, but now they were fifty thousand years old and hunting.

Running, he felt a weight impact against his left leg, immediately followed by a burning sensation behind his knee. Again the weight, the strike, and a new burning. And he realized with horror that one of the dogs was trying to sever the tendon, hamstring him. He slashed at the animal with his knife, missed.

A snarling shadow moved ahead, tripping him, and he stumbled forward out of control, fell, rose quickly, and went on.

Another heavy impact, throwing him off-stride—*I cannot fall down again*—and then there was a new hot pain on his left calf. Terrible things were happening to his body.

A blow just below his knee and he was down and skidding through the mud. He rolled over while still sliding, heard an evil snarl, felt a weight on his chest. A dog's head filled his field of vision. A hideous, surreal mask outlined against the pale sky, ears laid back, eyes slitted, upper lip peeled to expose the long, gleaming canine teeth. A hissing and slavering. A musty smell, dry and sour like mildewed wool. He instinctively lifted his left arm, offered it, sacrificed it. The dog bit down hard halfway between his elbow and wrist. He heard himself screaming.

Screaming, he drove the butcher knife beneath his forearm and into the animal's throat. Its body convulsed, there was a warm spray of blood in his face, and then, choking, the dog staggered off into the darkness.

There was a blank area in his memory then, the loss of a minute or so, and then he became aware that he was gripping the other dog's collar with his left hand and, with mindless ferocity, driving the knife again and again into its side.

He limped down the trail for another hundred yards and then, certain that he would soon faint, he dropped to his hands and knees and crawled off into the thick brush.

TWENTY

It was dark in here, but above, through the intricate lacing of branches, he could see the moon and the luminous haze of the Milky Way.

He lightly rubbed his right fingertips over his left forearm; deep puncture wounds, raggedly edged holes that welled blood. To the bone, he thought; the dog had bitten clear through skin and flesh to the bone. He dipped his fingers inside the several tears in his trousers and felt the lacerations. Long, deep slashes, welted along the edges with the surrounding flesh already swollen hard. Two slashes on the rear of his left thigh above the knee; a very bad gash on his calf, torn open, with loose flaps of skin. Another on his left inner thigh below the groin.

His hands and wrists were covered with blood, his own and the dogs'. He could smell it, sweet and metallic, a slaughterhouse stink. His pulse fluttered in his ears like the rapid beating of wings. He was faint and nauseated, sleepily drifting as with a fever.

A dog began barking somewhere above, and other

dogs up and down the hills responded with barks and howls. The noise of brush crackling to the north. The blood on his wounds had a tacky feeling now; he was starting to coagulate. A rustling in the brush and then a metallic clicking: two distinct clicks followed by a long silence. Harry very close, just a few yards away judging by the sounds. The brush crackled again. He was coming this way. Another mosquito-whining silence interrupted by the clicking noise, *click-click,* a pause, *click-click,* pause, *click-click.* Harry thumbing back the revolver's hammer, slowly drawing it through half cock to full cock; then lowering the hammer and cocking it again. Very close. Psych-war.

"Any dog-killing rabbits hereabouts?" Harry asked softly.

David's muscles tensed. There was a sour taste on the back of his tongue.

The brush rustled once more and there was a subtle change in the light, a new huge shadow materializing ten feet away. *Click-click.* He could hear Harry's breathing. *Click-click.*

"Bunny, bunny," he crooned. "Here, bunny." And then he laughed quietly.

A few more paces this way and Harry would step on him. He dared not move.

"*Hasenpfeffer,*" Harry whispered. "I know you're in here, *hasenpfeffer.*"

David tightened his grip on the wooden handle of the knife. If Harry moved a few steps closer . . .

Click-click. "I'm going to flush you, Brer *Hasen-pfeffer.*"

David was conscious of his stink of sweat and blood, and he feared that Harry would be able to smell him too.

There was a tiny spray of sparks in the darkness like static electricity, again, and then a tiny, wavering blade of flame. Cigarette lighter. In the glow, David could see Harry's shadowed face, still calmly malicious, with a humorous quirk to the lips. A thin, silvery glint of light extended the full length of the revolver's barrel and then shrank as the angle changed. *Click-click.* Harry seemed to be staring directly at him over the flame.

Sees me, David thought wildly, thinking to desperately throw the knife at him, but Harry's expression had not altered, there was no flicker of surprise or recognition.

A curse and the light went out. Burned fingers. And now, his night vision gone, David felt immersed in a total blackness that seemed to whirl around him. A dizzy spin, retinal flashes. Waiting. Two minutes, three.

And then Harry moved past him and went crashing through the underbrush. He zigzagged south, stopping periodically to murmur a few words, and then went on again. Finally he was gone.

David didn't know if he fainted then or just fell asleep, but he was awakened by a sharp crack. He opened his eyes. Nothing, and then a dull popping sound up high and a sudden glare as a small white sun was ignited overhead. The little sun swung like a clock pendulum as it descended. Parachute flare. A volley of cracks, an oddly harmonic combination of whistles, and then more popping sounds as a dozen little suns blossomed in the vast darkness above. The lights were queerly cold and flat, dimensionless, but they drew color out of the grass and leaves, etched the woods as in a silverpoint. Hissing, the balls of fire descended. And from below he could hear voices, laughter, the cracking of brush.

David lifted his wrist: 1:40 A.M. He had only slept for about thirty minutes. He was stiff, sick, thirsty. A spongy crust had formed over his wounds.

Flares, for God's sake. A long line of beaters. He rolled over, lay prone for a time, and then slowly and stiffly stood erect. Dizziness, nausea. His ankle felt frozen, the joint firmly locked. Jesus, I don't know if I can run anymore.

He limped out to the path. A long line of lights were moving uphill toward him, at least fifty lights strung out from north to south. Men with flashlights. Noise, raucous voices, continual crashing sounds, dogs barking, a transistor radio somewhere along the line playing ranchero music. The lights appeared to be spaced about fifteen or twenty yards apart, and were no more than seventy yards below him now. Parachute flares bloomed overhead like bizarre flowers.

David's impulse was to run uphill wildly, hysterically flee the noise and the lights and the men. But he knew that that was what they expected, wanted. There would be men stationed on the roads that traversed the hills above. This was like an animal drive, with beaters forcing the panic-stricken prey directly to the hunters' guns.

The thing was to penetrate the beater's line—freedom lay on the other side.

David returned to the woods and began climbing a tall tree. His wounds reopened; he could feel the scabs break and the warm, wet flow of blood. The bark was sticky and had a tart, resinous scent. He stopped thirty feet above the ground, sat on a thick limb with his feet hanging down and his right arm hugging the trunk.

The men were close now. He saw a flashlight out on the path. Coming this way. A parachute failed to open some distance to the south and he watched the flare plummet into the trees. If it hadn't rained earlier tonight they would set the entire mountain on fire, burn down fifteen million dollars worth of houses, incinerate dozens of families. They might anyway. It was insane. He knew, if he somehow escaped, that he would eventually regard all of this as comical. But not now. No, they could not spend all of this money and effort, alienate every rich man in town, without having the corpse of a homicidal maniac to show for it.

Two men, one with a flashlight, entered the thicket below his tree. They cursed the thorns and insects, the heat and their sergeant. Just shadows. They stopped below and about twenty feet to the north, at about the same place Harry had waited. One of them lit a cigarette and idly flicked his flashlight beam among the trees.

"*Venga, hombre, venga,*" he said.

The other man did not reply.

"The mosquitoes in here are like vampire bats."

Light gradually increased as if a rheostat were slowly being turned up. The upper halves of the leaves shined silver. Night, false dawn, and then day. David looked up. A flare was descending almost directly overhead, a baseball-sized white radiance ringed by two distinct coronas. Rocking gently, sputtering, and spewing light.

He could clearly see the two men now. One standing, smoking a cigarette, and watching the flare float down; the other sitting on the ground, one boot off. Both small, dark men. Indians. Soldiers: they wore camouflaged fatigues and holstered sidearms.

The seated man had his boot on now and was lacing it. *Get up*, David thought, *go now!*

The parachute, snagged in the high branches of a nearby tree, began to swing. It burned phosphorescently, sizzling, spitting sparks, dimming.

Just before the flare died, the standing man cocked his head and looked up at David. Their eyes greeted and locked. Surprised, paralyzed, they stared at each other.

The flare dimmed further, spit a last few sparks, and died. The flashlight below was turned off.

"I saw him." A hoarse, frightened whisper.

"Saw who?"

"The gringo. Over there, up in that tree. Give me the carbine."

"You saw nothing."

"I saw him, I swear, Jesus, Mary, and Joseph, he's sitting right up there."

"Hermano, listen, you did not see anything."

"I did, he's—"

"Nothing!" And then in a coaxing tone: "If he really was there he would have killed us by now. Isn't that so?"

"No, by God, he is *here!*"

"'Mano, 'Mano, listen to me, he isn't here. And if the gringo is here, what will you do? Kill him?"

Silence. David closed his eyes and hugged the tree. It was out of his hands now.

"Who would you kill him for? Yourself?"

"I don't know."

"For the sergeant? The lieutenant? The captain? The colonel? The government? Would you kill a man for the government?"

A hesitation. "I don't think so."

"The gringo isn't here, I promise you that. But who is he? A poor miserable man like you and me, a scared devil who has to hide in trees. Would you shoot him out of his tree for the government?"

"I understand." A short laugh.

"The gringo isn't here, but if he was up in that tree, do you know what I would do? I would say, 'To God, gringo!'"

Laughter. "I would say, 'Good luck, you tree-climbing snake!'"

More laughter. "I would say, 'I hope you get it wet one more time before you die, gringo!'"

There was considerable noise as they gathered their equipment and then, laughing loudly, they went crashing through the brush.

TWENTY-ONE

He waited five minutes, long enough to let any more stragglers pass, then descended the tree and limped out to the path. He was very hot, burning up, but no longer perspiring. Dehydration. Fever. The pain of his ankle was excruciating, so intense that it nearly canceled the pain from his wounds. I can make it, he thought, but he really wasn't sure.

There was still a lot of noise up above, and lights, but it was quiet here now. He limped slowly down the trail. Bleeding. How much blood does the human body contain?

The path emerged from the woods a few hundred feet above the coastal highway. There was a long grassy slope, the two-lane blacktop, and then a roughly triangular plateau that dropped steeply into the sea.

He stopped and looked down through the brush: three canvas-covered army troop trucks, a jeep, a police black and white, and Harry's Mercedes Benz. Harry had gotten this insane manhunt going, of course; he'd called Vigil and Vigil had called out the goddamned Mexican Army.

Some of the vehicles had their lights on and he could see a few men in uniform, one playing with a walkie-talkie, Vigil in his rainbow silk suit, and Harry.

After a while the military vehicles and the police car left the area; they would be on their way into the hill to pick up the soldiers. Failed mission, so far.

The moon was bright enough to draw shadows from Vigil's and Harry's bodies, elongated facsimiles: they stood in the center of the road, talking and gesturing. David could hear their voices but was unable to make out the words. Harry lit a cigarette, waved toward the sea; then the two of them crossed the road and walked out onto the plateau. They went all the way to the cliff and stood there silhouetted against the sea and sky.

The cliffs were steep and about seventy feet high and there were huge rocks collected at the bottom. On stormy days the surf hit those rocks and geysered a hundred feet into the air. That was where the girl had been killed. A long time ago, it seemed, years.

A night like this: the indigo sea fracturing itself into parallel white lines of surf that crack like thunder on the rocks; moon and stars; white clouds stretching and flexing like swans; the rain-freshened scents of trees and grass and soil. He strangled her and threw her body down on the rocks. Good old Harry.

David stepped out of the woods and began limping down the grassy field toward the road. He couldn't run anymore. He wouldn't crawl. If the two men happened to turn now they would see him. Okay. No more running, no more fox and hounds. He kept going, fueled by an ice-cold rage, down the slope and over to the Mercedes. He opened the front passenger door and got in.

The keys were not in the ignition. Nor behind the visor or under the driver's seat. He found Harry's big .44 Magnum revolver in the glove compartment; apparently old Harry had thought it unwise to carry it while the cops were around. David opened the cylinder. It was fully loaded. All right then, play the cards you're dealt.

Vigil and Harry had turned and started back to the road. They were still a couple hundred feet away. Harry was talking loudly, ". . . but goddamn, Enrique, I never believed . . . "

David quickly slid over the seat into the back and lay on the floor, looking up, the revolver ready.

Closer now. Harry: ". . . cold-blooded son of a bitch to do a thing like that."

Vigil: "I see it all the time in my work. You can never really be sure what a friend, a neighbor, a relative is capable of doing."

The driver's door open, then the other; leather compressing, a jingle of keys, the smell of cigarette smoke.

". . . but I trusted the kid, I halfway adopted him."

Sure, Harry.

The engine started and there was a rush of air from the air-conditioning vents, warm at first and gradually cooling. David tensed; they certainly would smell him, his sweat and blood, his scared-animal stink. The car began moving.

Vigil: "Children, sweet old men, Christ-obsessed ladies, young men like David—I tell you, Harry, there is no explaining the moral putrefaction that—"

David swiftly rose and jammed the muzzle of the revolver into the hollow at the base of Vigil's head where the spinal cord fused with the lower brain; that point where the coup de grace was administered. Vigil stiffened, made a hissing sound through his teeth.

Harry, his face tinted green by the dash lights, turned abruptly. There was surprise in his expression, but no fear.

"Hey, kid, what the—"

"Shut up, Harry."

"Put that—"

"Shut up! Keep your eyes on the road and your hands on the steering wheel."

"Aren't you in enough trouble?" Vigil said.

"That's right, it can't get worse. Can it, you son of a bitch."

"Aw, Dave, come on, kid, we're only—"

"I told you to shut up, Harry. I can kill you because I'm nervous, I can kill you because I'm blind-mad at what you've done to me, but most likely I'll end up killing you simply because you talk too much."

Both men were silent then.

"Vigil, put your palms up on the dashboard. Okay. Where do you keep your gun—shoulder or belt holster?"

"I don't carry a gun."

"Tick-tock, Vigil, tick-tock."

"Shoulder."

David carefully reached over Vigil's shoulder, dipped his hand inside the jacket and removed a snub-nosed revolver. He stuck it into his left front trouser pocket.

"*Ley de fuga*, huh, Vigil? I guess maybe the law of flight should function both ways. You guys can shoot me, eureka, I can shoot you. Fair is fair. Quid pro quo. What's good for the goose—turn right on Avenida de las Americas, Harry, we're going to your place."

"Kid, the roads are swarming with cops and army. You'll never get through."

"Is that right?"

"No way you can make it through."

"Okay," David said.

"I mean it."

"I believe you. Pull the car over."

"I'm trying to help you."

"Sure. Pull the car over, Harry."

He slowed the Mercedes, eased it over onto the shoulder, and stopped.

"Get out, Dave. Start running again."

"You misunderstood. I'm going to kill you two and take the car."

Both men stared straight ahead through the windshield.

"Who wants to be first? Harry?"

"We can get through," Vigil said in a strained voice.

"Get out of the car, Harry, very slowly."

"I can get us *through*," Vigil said.

"Tell your friend that," David said.

"Harry, for Christ's sake, man, do what he says."

"He's bluffing. I know him, I've known him for two years. He's a punk."

"Keep talking," David said. "You're doing real good."

Vigil was moving his head back and forth, silently saying no, no, no . . .

"Now you'd better get out of here," Harry said, "before I take the gun away and whip your brains out with it."

David laughed. Harry was tough, he really was. It took guts to talk to a gun that way. This thing was spinning out of control now. It had to be settled.

"Vigil," he said, "keep your hands on the dash."

David slid down the seat and placed the muzzle of the revolver behind Harry's right ear. He slowly cocked the hammer as Harry had in the woods, so that there were two distinct, ominous clicks. "Remember earlier tonight," he said softly. "You couldn't pull the trigger. I'll pull it for you, *hasenpfeffer*." It seemed that a kind of electrical current passed back and forth through the steel conductor. Rage, hatred, fear, pressure and resistance, trembling and stillness—the gun was alive with their conflict. And just when David realized that yes, he could pull the trigger, and yes, he probably would, there was an exquisitely subtle variation in the tension and Harry softly whispered, "No."

"No," he said. "Don't," he said. "Please," he said.

Vigil exhaled explosively.

"Drive, Harry."

When they were well into the hills the headlights flashed on soldiers who stood or sat on the shoulders of the road. They went on past a parked army truck, the jeep, the police car, and then around a hairpin corner where the other army truck blocked the road. Harry had to brake hard to avoid a collision.

"It's up to you, Vigil," David said quietly, concealing the gun beneath his right thigh. "Harry? Your choice."

Three men crossed the headlight beams, one an officer who wore white gaiters, a white Sam Browne belt, and carried a swagger stick. His face looked like the moon, round and pale and cratered with old acne scars. He walked over to the driver's side, leaned over, glanced at Harry and Vigil, and then cocked his head to stare at David.

"We caught him, Colonel," Vigil said in Spanish.

The officer stared. Eyes like a lizard. No expression. A walking dead man, a zombie like Luis de Borbolla.

Still staring at David, the man said, "Do you require any assistance?"

"No."

"He isn't restrained."

"He is my prisoner, Colonel."

The man looked at Vigil no less coldly than he'd stared at David, then he straightened, whipped his swagger stick down on the car top, and backed away, saying, "Take him away then."

They passed a few more soldiers on the coiled road and then turned off onto Harry's seashell driveway.

"He knew," Vigil said.

"Knew what?"

"That we were your hostages."

"Perhaps."

"You're being very stupid, David."

"When was I smart?" he said furiously. "When I refused to run because I was innocent and innocent people don't go to jail? When you handcuffed me to the café table? When you slapped me around, Vigil? When I was rotting in that cesspool jail? Don't call me stupid, you bastard, not when I'm finally learning the rules to your game."

He got them out of the car without any trouble, and down the walk and through the iron gate into the pool area, and then Harry said, "Dave, that gun's empty."

The pool lights and a string of paper lanterns were burning. Harry and Vigil were walking side by side a few feet ahead of David.

"You know it's empty, kid, if anyone does—you threw the cartridges into the pool."

They reached the shallow end of the pool and Harry hesitated, nudged Vigil, and nodded toward the water.

"Shut up, Harry."

Vigil, seeing the shells in the water, whirled and lunged. David backhandedly chopped the revolver across Vigil's face, not swinging hard, a slap, but he had not calculated the force that the heavy gun would exert at the whip-end of his arm. Vigil's lower face gushed blood. He staggered back a few steps and fell hard on the pool apron.

Harry had moved aside, out of the firing line, and he was crouched, tense, and ready. But when he saw that there was no chance he relaxed, smiled, and nodded.

Vigil was sitting up now, spitting blood and bits of teeth into his cupped palms.

"That was nice, Harry," David said. "What do you call that—pawn sacrifice? Help your good friend into the house."

It appeared that there were no bones in Vigil's legs; he sagged back to the tiles several times, drooling blood, and then Harry dragged him erect and half carried him into the house.

David ordered them to lie spread-eagled on the living room floor with their hands against the north wall. Harry helped Vigil and then paused, looking sideways at the gun.

"You're begging for it."

"I got nothing to lose, kid."

"All right, lose your nothing now, then."

He smiled and shook his head. "Not yet." Big Harry, gruff as a bear with a paw full of thorns, but with a heart as big as all outdoors. Sentimental Harry, quick with a buck and a story, once nearly the biggest GM dealer in the Midwest.

"Down," David said.

TWENTY-TWO

David walked over to the liquor cabinet and removed a bottle of cognac and a bottle of ginger ale. Turning, he saw his reflection in a mirror and was horrified; he had lost at least twenty pounds in jail; his clothes were torn to shreds, and there was blood everywhere; a torn lump the size of an apple had risen where the dog had bitten his forearm; and his deeply sunken eyes were surrounded by flesh as black as soot. Portrait of a desperado—lock up the womenfolk.

He switched on all of the outside lights, pulled the drapes, carried the bottles over to a sofa, and sat down. There seemed to be no bottom to the cushions. He leaned back and stretched out his legs, permitted the softness to embrace him. Harry and Vigil were sprawled out on the floor a few yards away. Draped windows behind him, and then the pool area. To his right the big fireplace and the stairway leading to the upper floor; on his left another sofa, chairs, a big bookcase, a fine Zuñi painting. A big room, a comfortable room.

"Harold T-for-Tipton Rudd," David said. "Captain Enrique Vigil. Gentlemen: keep your mouths shut, your noses clean, and your thoughts pure, and we'll get along."

David drank half a quart of warm ginger ale and placed the bottle on the side table. Now that Harry and Vigil were more or less under control, now that he could relax for a while, there was a letdown and he experienced a vertiginous sliding sensation, like descending in an elevator with your eyes closed. Like being seasick: nausea, dizziness, and an overwhelming lassitude. His sweat was cold. He didn't know how long he could keep going this way, on pain and fear.

"Vigil," he said. "Harry killed the girl."

Harry, face down on the tiles, said, "He's full of shit."

There was a telephone on the side table. He lifted the receiver and dialed the medical clinic; no answer. He tried Pacheco's home number and told the servant who answered that one of the doctor's rich American patients wished to speak with him. It was an emergency. A long wait and then Pacheco's sleep-husky voice said, *"Digame?"*

"It's me."

"I guessed."

"I need additional medical care, Paco."

Pacheco laughed softly.

"Harry's Doberman pinschers chewed on me."

He laughed again. "And they got sick? Sorry, I am not a veterinarian."

"Vigil needs medical attention too."

"Vigil?"

"I'm at Harry's place. I've got two guns, one big gun and one small gun. Harry and Vigil are my hostages."

A silence. "And you shot Vigil?"

"No, not yet."

"Well, shoot him. Shoot Harry too."

"Are you coming?"

"Will you shoot me?"

"Probably not."

"It sounds like fun, but . . . "

"Don't forget your satchel."

"Shall I bring the cops?"

"No, thanks, I've got a cop here."

"Maybe I should bring more."

"Sure, okay. Bring a priest too, Paco."

Pacheco laughed again. "I'm on my way, Captain America."

David hung up the telephone, took a drink of cognac, and put the bottle on the table. God, he was beat.

"Vigil," he said, "I'm sorry about your teeth. But not very. They weren't *nice* teeth."

The room slid out of focus. It was sharply defined, a familiar and coherent pattern, and then it just fell to pieces, dissolved into abstract forms and wandering colors. He slept briefly. He was there in the room with them and then he was gone, alone in darkness and oblivion, and then he came back. In and out, a three second nap, though it seemed much longer. He awakened when his head lowered beyond a certain point and the heavy revolver began to slip from his grasp.

He dozed that way two or three more times, and then heard footsteps outside, a brisk rapping on the door. "Paco?"

"Yes."

"Are you alone?"

"Just me and my guardian angel."

"The angel stays outside."

Pacheco came in slowly, carrying his black satchel, and kicked the door closed with his heel.

"Don't point that thing at me," he said.

"Lock the door."

"It's bad manners to point."

"Lock it."

Paco turned the lever on the doorknob and then closed the safety chain. He studied David's bloody, torn clothing, the wound on his forearm, his eyes, and then glanced across the room.

"What's wrong with Vigil?"

"His teeth fell out."

"David, did you know that there is an army outside this house?"

"On the roads, you mean?"

"No, no, outside here, surrounding this place."

"Did you bring them?"

"They were here when I arrived. They let me through when I told them that you had called me, that Captain Vigil was hurt."

"Okay."

"A berserk colonel is considering a commando action."

David smiled.

Pacheco stared at him. "David, did you hear me?—the army is out there!"

"I'll review the troops later, Paco."

Pacheco unzipped his satchel, removed a thermometer from its sterile container, and shook it down.

"You intend to take my temperature?"

"David, did you summon me in my professional capacity or because you need a fourth for bridge? Here, hold it under your tongue."

He carried his satchel across the room and kneeled next to Vigil.

David cautiously peeled back an edge of the drape—snipers?—and looked outside. Silence, no movement. But of course they would not enter the brightly lit pool area. Not until the berserk colonel launched his commando assault. Christ, this thing just kept escalating, getting bigger and more complex and crazier; it grew like a cancer and would probably end with the burn of tear gas and commandos crashing through the windows and the rattle of automatic weapons fire. David knew that he would fight back. They had declared war against him, hadn't they?

Pacheco was on his feet now. "Vigil is concussed," he said.

"Bad?"

"Hard to say." He set his bag on the floor, reached out, and removed the thermometer from David's mouth.

"Do you have to point that gun at me?"

"I think so, yes. Sorry." He realized now that Paco

had been scared ever since entering the room; he was trying to carry on in his usual jaunty, obnoxious style, but fear was evident in the tension around his mouth and a certain jerkiness in his motions.

"You have a temperature of one hundred and two. Not good. Very bad in fact. We've got to attack the infection. Are you allergic to penicillin?"

"No."

"You need a huge dose. And a little morphine for the pain."

"No, no morphine."

"Codeine, then."

"No pain killers, Paco. Pain is the only thing that keeps me going."

"I'll clean and dress your wounds." He shook his head. "Fighting with the other dogs beneath a full moon. Did you establish supremacy, are you the leader of the pack now?"

"I killed them."

Pacheco stared at him. "You have turned into a fucking maniac."

"I had to. And you know, Paco, I am beginning to suspect that mania is the only thing that works."

A nod, a wry smile. "How you are the master and I am the student."

"Will you go outside and try to persuade the berserk colonel not to move for a while yet? Tell him that you believe that you can convince me to surrender."

"And can I convince you of that?"

"You can certainly try."

Pacheco went into one of the other rooms and returned with a pillow case. "I had better show a white flag," he said.

"You trust Mexicans with guns more than I do."

"I don't trust anyone with guns." He opened the door and, standing behind the wall, waved the pillow case in the doorway before stepping outside.

David felt himself letting down again, sort of deflating mentally and physically. Doctor Pacheco had watched him with a steady, flat, appraising stare—he knew how badly off David was.

"Cooking something up, guys?" David said.

Harry and Vigil had been very quiet. Too silent, too still, far too passive even for men hoping to avert violent death. Those two were not a pair of hysterical clerks. They were not submissive men. No doubt they had been whispering to each other, conspiring. He should have separated them earlier. Let it go. He would not say anything now. Too many threats and they would begin to fear him less. Threats were an indication of weakness, of uncertain will.

It seemed that Paco had been gone for a long time. Scheming with the troops? Stalling, just letting time pass while knowing that David was approaching total collapse? Or maybe he was simply too frightened to return. He felt himself drifting off toward an unconsciousness that was more than mere sleep.

"Harry," he said. "Kill any girls lately?"

No reply.

They were up to something, all right. Plans, designs,

tactics. When this happens, you do this and I'll do that. Vigil again would be the one to expose himself first. Persuasive old Harry would see to that.

David drank some of the cognac. "Blown any investigations recently, Captain Vigil?"

Sounds outside, a knock on the door.

"Paco?"

"Yes."

"Alone?"

"And very lonely."

"All right, come in. Slowly."

Pacheco came in and closed and locked the door. He was very pale.

"You've got guts," David said.

"I'd like to keep them in the original container."

"What did they tell you?"

"You've got until sunrise."

"Okay." David did not believe it; they would make promises of course, but wouldn't necessarily keep them. No reason why they should. Still, he felt that this meant that they intended to grant him a little time, anyway, while they waited to see if Paco succeeded in his persuasion or his treachery. No, not treachery. Paco would be acting correctly; after all it was he, David, who was the murder suspect, the jail escapee, the man threatening the lives of others. Paco had to see it that way and naturally hoped to see it ended.

"I'll patch you up now," he said, lifting his satchel onto the coffee table. "Give you some shots. Penicillin and tetanus."

"No shots, Paco."

"But David, you—"

"No buts, Doctor. Move across the room, that way. Further, over there by the other sofa. Sit down on it if you like. Now, Vigil and Harry—I want you both to sit up and face me. Turn over. Okay. Now sit up with your backs against the wall and your legs stretched straight out on the floor. Hands on your thighs. Go ahead."

They obeyed very slowly, sullenly, resisting all the way, testing his temper and will. Vigil's lower face was swollen to twice its normal size and was caked with blood. There was fresh blood on his grotesquely swollen lips. His dark eyes appeared alert, though, quick and wary. Harry affected boredom; he sprawled lazily, his eyes hooded, smirking at David.

"Okay," David said, "let's end this one way or another."

"David . . . "

"Quiet, Paco. Now Vigil, who told you that you would find the girl's veil in my room?" He waited. "Vigil?"

"Harry." He wiped blood from his mouth with the back of his hand.

"Right. Harry has been helping you with your investigation all along, hasn't he? He's been your eyes and ears in the American community. Feeding you information—lies—about me. But probably it wasn't that raw, Harry would be sad and reluctant while he sold me out, hints and hesitations, frowns and . . . Vigil?"

"No."

"Vigil, the truth."

"It wasn't exactly like that."

David grinned.

"I'm getting tired of this crap," Harry said.

"Sorry I busted all of your front teeth, Vigil. I'll bet your mouth hurts like hell. But wasn't it clever the way Harry conned you into believing that the gun was empty? You saw the bullets in the pool and jumped me. I came very, very close to killing you. Cute Harry. A nice guy, a fellow you can trust."

"This is my home," Harry said. "And in about two minutes I'm going to walk upstairs and go to bed."

"I came up here tonight after seeing you, Paco. Harry had a gun—this gun—up against his head. But he couldn't kill himself. We talked. He admitted killing the girl. Told me all about it. Made it sound like the kind of thing you did at fraternity parties."

Harry was smiling faintly. Pacheco looked interested.

"Before I ran from here, though, before Harry could kill me, he gave me some things, money, some of his wife's jewelry. Paco, look under the sofa you're sitting on. Go ahead."

Pacheco got down on his hands and knees, looking beneath the sofa, and then scooped out the things David had hidden there.

"There's a heavy silver ring in there, with a crab insignia."

Pacheco sorted through the items, removed the ring, and stood up.

"Harry wanted those things found on my corpse. That ring belonged to the girl. I saw it on her finger. Maybe you did too, Paco."

"Yes."

"If that ring had been found in my possession . . . Well, there wouldn't be much doubt, would there? The veil in my room, the ring in my pocket. I don't know why Harry kept the stuff. Maybe as ghastly mementos, as you said, Vigil. Or maybe for use in framing someone—me, if it came to that."

Harry's smile widened; he was showing his teeth now. Very relaxed, superior. Vigil had closed his eyes and was gently rubbing his lips with the fingertips of his left hand.

Now David felt himself slipping away again, drifting down into a dark, velvety softness. He gritted his teeth and fought it, gradually beat it, but came back weaker than before, and with an awareness that his story was not convincing. It was the truth but appearances counted more. Harry was the solid, substantial, and square citizen, while David was viewed as an exile, a fugitive from a U.S. felony charge, lobster poacher, and tennis bum . . . He needed proof and there wasn't any. Nothing that even looked like evidence.

He heard a sound upstairs, definite but not loud. The others pretended not to hear it. He smiled at them. Action would soon commence.

"Paco," he said, "are you Harry's physician?"

"I have been."

"And have you treated him for any complaint recently?"

He hesitated.

"Forget your professional ethics for a moment, if you have any."

"I haven't seen Harry lately as his physician, but I've heard he visited another doctor, Hererra. For what, I don't know."

"Paco, you told me that you had been treating the girl for a venereal disease."

Paco watched him, alert, intelligent, moving ahead.

"Yes."

"Are there various strains of VD?"

Pacheco nodded. "That's right. This is a fairly new strain, common in the States, particularly on the West Coast, but rare in Mexico. It's very resistant to antibiotics."

David didn't know if Pacheco was telling the truth or just trying to help him.

"So," he said, "if Hererra's records show that Harry has been treated for the same strain of venereal disease as the girl . . ."

Harry was not smiling now. "Kidneys," he said, "Hererra was treating me for that."

Vigil turned to look at him.

"Okay, okay, shit," Harry said with a little laugh. "So I picked up a dose. No more than a bad cold, right? But that doesn't prove anything."

"David," Pacheco said urgently, "give me the gun. Please, give it to me now, it's going to start soon."

"Vigil?" David said.

"I might consider reopening the investigation," Vigil said wearily.

"Hey, what is this?" Harry said. "Blow-smoke-in-Harry's-ear night?"

Pacheco crossed the room and held out his hand.

"How do you think the accident of similar venereal disease would go over in court?" Harry asked.

"David. Give me the gun."

"What bullshit!"

David did not want to surrender the revolver, but then he remembered that he still had Vigil's compact gun in his pocket.

"Not even the Mexican courts would indict me on that," Harry was saying. "But I have a family, friends, a position, even an accusation could ruin me."

Pacheco accepted the revolver and started toward the stairway.

"Paco," David cried, "don't go over there with a gun in your hand!"

The night exploded then, shattered into pieces. It all happened within ten seconds, all at once really, but each action seemed isolated, unrelated to all the others. David, delirious with fever, could not link the separate details into a complete whole. He perceived each part of the violent choreography as possessing equal significance; the ringing of the telephone was no less important than the crack of gunfire, death.

Paco, warned not to approach the stairway, stopped in the middle of the room. And Harry, his face oddly red and swollen, blood-engorged, was rising from the floor. (Vigil futilely raised a hand to stop him—a languid wave.)

The telephone rang. A signal, of course, and a distraction. The outside lights were turned off. Harry had almost reached Pacheco, and his strength and fury seemed to occupy the room, claim it. An object thumped down the stairs and rolled out into the room, a dark canister that spun eccentrically and spewed a yellow-white smoke.

David hurled himself to the floor and tried to draw Vigil's snub-nosed revolver, but the hammer snagged on his pocket. The telephone rang again. The room was fogged with smoke now, a sharp, bitter stink that closed his throat and seared his eyes and sinuses. He managed to tear Vigil's revolver free of his pocket, but Harry had taken the big gun away from Pacheco now. Paco was falling. David could not tell if he had been hurt. The telephone rang again.

Now Harry turned, a vague dark figure in the spiraling smoke, and he lifted the gun and fired at David. A red spurt, a roar that seemed to never end, increasing and continuing, thundering over the ringing of the telephone and the sharper cracking of Vigil's snub-nose and the stuttering chatter of the automatic weapons outside in the pool area.

The gun bucked against David's grip five times, and Harry was hit once, twice, but he remained standing. The window drapes were twitching now and pictures falling from the wall and plaster spraying through the room.

Another object bounced down the stairs and wobbled out into the room. This one was elliptical. Harry was going down now, he had been hit by David's fire and hit again and again by the automatic weapons fire pouring in through the windows.

The egg-shaped object rocked gently on the floor. The telephone was ringing. David hurled his revolver across the room and sprawled out flat on the floor.

There was a thunderclap and the vibrations beat like fists on his body. A vacuum followed the concussion; he could not breathe. The telephone was still ringing.

Sirens howled like wolves off in the night. The area around the swimming pool was chaotic. Soldiers and police milled about, firemen dragged a hose along the pool apron toward the house (flames lunged behind the shattered windows), and curious neighbors in bathrobes and slippers, silent and avid, gathered in small groups. A confusion with undercurrents of panic in it, but David was now encapsulated in his own dreamy calm, aware yet indifferent—enough, he thought, no more, I quit.

He was lying on a chaise lounge. He vaguely recalled being carried out of the house. And now dawn was not far off; the air was cool, smelling of sea and smoke, and the stars had dimmed.

Vigil was lying on another chaise a few feet away. His eyes were closed, but he was breathing steadily.

"Captain?" David said.

No reply.

"Son of a bitch."

David closed his eyes for a time and when he opened them he saw Dr. Pacheco, gnomish and smiling cynically, staring down at him. There were many cuts on Paco's face, and his shirt was slashed and bloody.

"What happened to you?"

"Flying glass."

"We lost the war, huh, Paco?"

"You might say that. Or you could say that our sacrifices were not in vain, we persevered in a noble cause and achieved peace with honor."

"Harry?"

"Slain in battle, alas."

"Well, I'm not sure, but I guess I'm sorry about that."

"*C'est la guerre.* Do you want a painkiller?"

"No."

"Take it easy. We'll get you and Vigil to the hospital soon."

"How is Vigil?"

"Ask him."

The fire in the house had been extinguished and now the firemen were dragging the hose back along the tiles. A drunk man in a bathrobe was wandering from group to group, saying, "Have you seen Elaine? She hasn't been home. My God, was Elaine in there?"

"Vigil," David said. "I want to go home but I don't have the fare. Deport me soon, okay? By air."

Vigil opened his eyes and lay silently for a time staring at the sky, and then, speaking very softly and tenderly through his broken teeth and swollen mouth, he said, "You are going back to jail. You won't see daylight for five years."

"The situation has changed, Captain."

"Perhaps I shall kill you."

"I demand a public admission of error in my unjust arrest and imprisonment. All charges against me must be dropped, and my name expunged from the records. I want to be deported back to the States, by air, as soon as I'm released from the hospital. And I want your personal word that Chucho Aguilar won't be charged, or even annoyed, for helping me."

Vigil hissed air through his teeth; it might have been a kind of laugh.

The sky had paled with false dawn, dimming the glare from the artificial light and obliterating the stars. On the far side of the pool three soldiers, casually gesturing with their automatic rifles, were talking quietly in some toneless Indian language. The firemen were gone. And then two men bearing a stretcher, staggering beneath the weight, carried Harry's body down along the pool apron and out through the iron spear gate. The corpse had mostly been covered by a bloody white bedsheet, but David had seen a few wisps of hair, the bald spot on the crown of Harry's head, and a big white—unnaturally white—ear. Harry drained of blood. The image of that convoluted white ear lingered in David's mind.

Doctor Pacheco, smoking a cigar, still jaunty, approached the lounge chairs. "Okay, invalids," he said. "The press is laying siege outside the walls. There's even a guy who claims to be a stringer for *Time* magazine. The army is telling them lies, the police are telling them lies—what do we tell them?"

Vigil licked his bloody lips. "Nothing."

"Everything," David said. "About how I was unjustly, illegally imprisoned and brutally tortured."

Pacheco grinned around his cigar.

"And how Harry Rudd, a decent, prominent American citizen was murdered in his own home by a bunch of fascist thugs. And that isn't all."

"I bet it isn't," Pacheco said.

"The world will be appalled by my story. Americans by the millions will refuse to visit this country."

Pacheco nodded. "That might be the best thing that ever happened down here." He looked at Vigil. "Captain?"

Vigil glanced at David, turned away. "All right," he said.

"All right what?" David asked.

"I agree to your demands."

"What were my demands? Let Dr. Pacheco hear them."

"We shall—issue a statement acknowledging your innocence of the murder."

"And exonerate me for escaping from jail."

"And that. And you will be deported at our expense."

"By air."

"Yes."

"What else, Vigil?"

"The Aguilar boy will not be bothered."

"What else?"

"What do you mean?"

"Aren't you going to give me your *personal* apology too?"

"No. Never."

Pacheco was grinning.

"I want to talk to that *Time* stringer, Paco. I want to talk to CBS, to Amnesty International, to everyone."

Vigil inhaled deeply, held it, and then exhaling, said, "I-am-sorry-David."

"What a pair of jerks," Pacheco said. "Hang on, jerks, the stretchers will be here at any second."

"Never mind a stretcher for me," David said. "I can walk."

JACKSTRAW

MUNDIAL

I assembled the rifle and secured the telescope to its mounting. The bolt worked with a smooth metallic *snick*. The rifle smelled of steel and oil and wood polish and, faintly, burnt gunpowder. It was the smell of my past, the smell of my future.

At dawn I moved to an open window. A woman, wrapped and hooded by a ropy shawl, walked diagonally across the paving stones toward the cathedral. She flushed a flock of pigeons which swirled like confetti before settling. A limping yellow dog came out of the shadows and began chasing the birds. He had no chance. He knew it; the pigeons knew it. Finally the dog shamefully limped away down an alley.

I went into the bathroom and washed my face with tap water the color of weak tea. The cracked mirror fractured my image into half a dozen oblique planes, like a Cubist portrait, and gave my eyes a crazed slant.

Sunlight had illuminated the parapet and pediment of the National Palace. People were filtering into the great plaza now: churchgoers, early celebrants, lottery ticket salesmen and shoeshine boys, beggars, men pushing wheeled charcoal braziers and food carts. An old man filled colored balloons from a helium tank. Boys kicked around a soccer ball. Policemen in pairs cruised like sharks among schools of bait fish. Now and then I heard the voices of people passing by in the corridor. A door slammed, a woman laughed, elevator doors hissed open. This was for many an ordinary workday; they would observe the ceremony from their office windows, witnesses to pseudo history.

Blue smoke uncoiling from charcoal fires hung in the air like spiral nebulae. The cathedral's copper-sheathed dome, green with verdigris, glowed like fox-fire in the hazy sunlight. At ten o'clock the church bells again tolled, a loud off-pitch clanging whose vibrations continued—like ghosts of sound—to hum in the air ten seconds after the clangor had ceased. Two cops dragged a rowdy young man into the shade beneath the east side colonnade and began beating him with their clubs.

Members of a band were gathering on the steps of the National Palace. Spiders of sunlight shivered over their brass instruments. They wore royal blue uniforms with big brass buttons and coils of gold braid. There were about forty of them and they all looked like admirals.

There was a great cheer as four Cadillac limousines entered the plaza from the north. They moved at a funereal pace. You could not see anything through the tinted windows. Rockets were launched from the four corners of the square; there were prolonged whistles and parabolas of smoke, and then the rockets exploded into stringy flowers of red and yellow and blue.

The limousines halted in front of the palace. Lackeys rushed forward to open the doors. The American candidates, old Hamilton Keyes and Rachel Leah Valentine, exited from one of the limos; the four missionaries from another; and government big shots, in black silk suits and snappy military uniforms, emerged from the other two cars.

The band started playing the country's national anthem. Three fighter jets in close formation roared low over the square, rattling windows and churning the smoke, and when the noise of the jets faded I could again hear the music and the cheering crowd.

*   *   *

The President of the Republic welcomed the people, welcomed the liberated missionaries, welcomed the distinguished American political candidates, welcomed a new day of national reconciliation and international amity. The crowd applauded. The band played a lively *pasodoble,* "Cielo Andaluz," as if the president had just cut ears and tail from a bull.

The American vice-presidential candidate ended her speech with a series of rhetorical spasms.

"Now!" she cried.

"*Ahora!*" the dark-haired girl near her repeated in Spanish.

Feedback from the speakers situated around the square resonantly echoed the last syllable of each word.

"And tomorrow!"

"*Y mañana!*"

I crawled forward and propped the rifle barrel on the window sill.

"Forever!"

"*Siempre!*"

I placed the intersection of the telescope's crosshairs between Rachel's breasts.

"All of the people!"

"*Toda la gente!*"

"Everywhere!"

"*En todo el mundo!*"

The crowd loved her.

Rachel Leah Valentine arched her back, spread her arms wide and—ecstatic, cruciform—gazed up at the incandescent blue sky.

I gently squeezed the trigger.

Now. Let it all come down.

CPSIA information can be obtained at www.ICGtesting.com
Printed in the USA
BVOW031129110713

325696BV00001B/65/P